WHY GO ON A TUESDAY?

WHY GO ON A TUESDAY?

a novel by

Carter Wilson

Bankilal Books

WHY GO ON A TUESDAY?
Published by Bankilal Books

Library of Congress Control Number: 2023943815

ISBN (paperback): 9781662943393
eISBN: 9781662943409

For Thomas, who loves a good *servicio de té*

"The cave surely takes people."

"If you did something there it is sure your spirit
would stay in the cave."

-- Francisca Hernández Hernández Tzotzil story teller

A NOTE

I have named and even occasionally made characters of some real people in a story which is otherwise entirely fictional. The living "real" will certainly recognize themselves, and the shades of those who have gone along to the *mas allá* will doubtless take comfort from the fact that I have attributed nothing to them they did not say or do during their time here below (or above).

AN ACKNOWLEDGEMENT

Thanks to the late Robert M. Laughlin and Francisca Hernández Hernández for the book's epigrams, which come from their <u>Mayan Tales from Chiapas, Mexico; "I Know Best" and Other Tzotzil Tales</u>

From the moment Maryanne Fort announced she was thinking of going back to southern Mexico on a visit, her grown children united against her.

"What would you do there anyway?" said Helen, the eldest.

"You mean alone, without your father?" said Maryanne. "I'd manage somehow."

"That's not what I meant, Mother. I know you could <u>manage</u>. You managed for Dad there all those years, didn't you?"

Maryanne nodded, but she noticed Helen glancing up briefly at the mantel.

"Dad" was Giles Fort, the anthropologist, who had died in September. Now, the Monday after Thanksgiving, mother and daughter were having coffee in Maryanne's Wilmette living room. A heavy snow had fallen overnight and the relentless dazzle of the band of sun across the carpet made Maryanne's temples and in fact her whole forehead ache. She had had Giles's ashes back for almost four weeks but hadn't yet told the children what she planned to do with them.

At his college fraternity house ('Before I became a serious person,' as Giles would say), the brothers would congregate for after-dinner smokes around the fireplace in what they grandly called The Lounge. The game was to flick their cigarette butts up and get them to land in the trophy cup under the stuffed moose's big leathery nose. Giles's best friend from those years, a man who later became a TV producer, found old-time photographic flash powder somewhere and loaded the trophy with it. The next brother to get lucky tripped an explosion which singed off most of Mr. Moose's hair and set a fire which threatened to burn down the dear old Sigma Chi itself.

The Fort children loved this story, the little ones becoming nearly hysterical over their sometimes stiff-backed dad using the word "butt" so freely. Later, before Giles knew he was actually dying, he would indicate the mantel at the Wilmette house and say, "When the time comes, just put me up there in some vase or other and you can flick your butts at the old man in perpetuity."

"So you'd just go to San Cristóbal for a while?"

When Maryanne didn't immediately respond, Helen prompted, "Mom?"

"Yes, that's right," Maryanne said. "Though what I really want is to see Manantiales one more time."

San Cristóbal de Las Casas, seventy miles east and 6,000 feet above the Chiapas state capital at Tuxtla, was the jumping off place for what Giles sometimes called, with no disrespect, 'Indian Country,' Manantiales the Tzeltal Maya-speaking community back in the mountains where the Forts first worked. When they started there over 40 years ago, Manantiales was a day-and-a-half up out of San Cristóbal by horse or mule. Now Maryanne had heard the construction of a road put the village only three hours from the nearest cybercafé.

"I'd like to be the one to tell them about your father," Maryanne added.

The little pursing of Helen's lips was so brief it hardly happened. Do children not understand, especially grown ones, that a mother will still read even their smallest signs of resistance? Did Helen really resent the fact that the people of Manantiales were still close enough to Maryanne's heart that she would refer to them simply as "them?"

Maryanne had been about to say she was thinking she might leave at least a portion of Giles's ashes in Manantiales. But now she decided to put off any further announcements, at least for today.

She and Giles had tried to bill fieldwork to the kids as an extended version of good old American family camping. But all four children ended up disliking village life intensely, and the summers they spent in San Cristóbal only slightly less. Helen and Giles Junior were eloquent about the particulars of how unhappy they had been. Cecile, third in line and at home in California now, would start into a recollection which sounded as though it was going to turn out pleasant enough, but then some brilliantly-colored, mortally-venomous Central American spider would come gyrating down into the anecdote and you were left with the impression that Cecile lived every moment her thoughtless parents forced her to linger in Manantiales in mortal terror. Rennie, the youngest, simply denied any memory of Manantiales, though she had spent what would have been her first-grade year there, and her mother had Kodak-bright mental pictures of Rennie flying kites at the top of a long meadow and, down by the gray river, studiously trapping dragon flies and attempting with precocious delicacy to put them in bottles without damaging their wings.

Just as Maryanne had given up trying to talk her offspring out of their grudge against Chiapas, she had also long since abandoned hope any of them would ever become capable of imagining what an eye-opener Manantiales had been for her and Giles when they were very young Chicago grad students in the late 1950s. Neither of them had ever been more than briefly out of the Midwest before they set off for Mexico. They arrived in San Cristóbal newly married and certainly in love but actually not yet entirely accustomed to one another. They were guided in to Manantiales the first time on horseback by a functionary of the Mexican Secretariat of Education. There was a federal primary school in the village center, but at the time no teacher, at least none in evidence. The functionary introduced them to a couple of men whose first names he seemed to know and then prepared to leave. Maryanne could still remember the curious crowd that gathered, the anxious faces, and the government man's barking condescension, the relentless rat-tat-tat of his Spanish. *Here, these are inspectors from the outside who are working for us. They will sleep in the teacher's quarters at the school and pay you something for their food. Treat them well.*

And if you cheat them, I personally will hear about it. When he left he took with him the little horses they had ridden in on.

It was already nearly twilight then. The vacant teacher's room turned out to be a dank cement cell with only one narrow metal-frame bed. No way the two gringos would fit on it. They shook out some straw mats and propped the mattress against the wall as a kind of bolster, Giles zipped their sleeping bags together and they passed the first night on the floor clinging together praying the mice careening along the rafters overhead wouldn't miss a step and land on their heads.

Sometimes Maryanne wondered if any of her offspring had ever looked at <u>Cornucopia, living a Maya life</u>, their original book about Manantiales. To the publisher's surprise, it had skipped over out of the academic groove and had a bit of popular success. Though the book came out under Giles's name, Maryanne had done a large portion of the thinking and some of the writing and had edited the whole thing. She remembered long tense hours trying to cut down Giles's description of their fieldwork conditions, not because the section was dry but because Giles wrote so exuberantly about the endlessly changing beauty of Manantiales, the discretion, grace, and canniness of the people, even waxing poetic over the smoky rich taste of blue corn tortillas when they come fresh off the comal.

"When?"

"When what? Oh, when might I go?" Maryanne thought. "In a week or so. I want to be home in time for Christmas. Cecile and her boys are coming, you know. We'll have it here at the house if that's all right."

But it appeared at least for the time being nothing was going to be all right with Eldest Daughter. Among other quarrels, she was barely speaking with Junior, presumably over the way he was working on Dad's estate. Or <u>not</u> getting to work on it, or something. When Helen asked with pretended equanimity what her brother and his wife were doing for the holidays, Maryanne got up, put their cups on the tray and started for the kitchen. Turning back at the doorway into the hall, she said, "They're going to Vail."

Helen picked up her pocketbook, futzed in it, wedged it back down between her hip and the chair arm. Though her attempt to look blank was ineffective, Maryanne couldn't help smiling. From early on, age three or so, Helen had seemed to sense it when the apparently unrelated decisions of others impinged on <u>her</u> dignity. Giles's mother, a farm wife in Indiana, would lean down to her little granddaughter and say, "Why the bee-stung lip, honey?" And though Grandma Fort's tone was friendly enough, she would often reduce the already-affronted Helen to tears.

In the kitchen while Maryanne rinsed up Helen lit into Junior. What a showoff, flaunting his money like that. Vail was entirely for phonies and fat cats, she announced.

Maryanne had to suppress a laugh. Helen was married to an investment banker and lived a block across Sheridan Road from the Lake in the south end of Winnetka. Both of her boys attended North Shore Country Day, a private school in the town that supported New Trier, often ranked among the best public schools in the nation. So who exactly was calling who a fat cat?

This new squabbling among themselves Maryanne figured to be the way the children had found to express their feelings about the way their father died. Giles had just retired--to a lot of tooting and endowing of book prizes and graduate scholarships in his name--when colon cancer appeared for the first time. An operation, then a second one, and the all-clear signal. Giles settled in to write a book in his newly rewired and refurnished study at home. Then metastasis, something in his throat, painfully blown-up lymph glands, and quite suddenly the only remaining hope appeared to be a new treatment they were trying in Houston. The Chicago-area children rallied admirably. They spelled Maryanne at the hospital, came to visit when Dad was in bed at home. Rennie, not only the youngest but also the most saturnine by nature, found a way to match the cheeriness Giles continued to broadcast with an even-tinnier version of her own. One evening in one of the endless waiting rooms they came to inhabit, her chirping finally grated on Junior. 'Where do you get your optimism, Sis?' he asked. Rennie pushed back her big mass of blond hair and replied, 'It's my new product. I'm calling it **Hope-on-a-Rope.**'

Cecile planned to meet her parents in Houston and take her turn helping out. But they never got that far. Giles was suddenly weak, then feeble, sleeping 20 hours a day, then being wheeled cold out the door by two men in ill-fitting jackets with vodka on their breath, all in a matter of a few weeks.

Helen announced she was going home. Maryanne followed her out and down the back steps. After the snowfall, a general chilling had come up and a sprightly wind from the direction of the Lake. Cold had turned the new snow crunchy. Both women gripped the handrail.

"Do you remember the business in Manantiales about the wake and the widow having to name her new intended before her husband's body could leave the house?"

"You know I don't remember much at all anymore about that place, Mother," Helen said, her voice tired and flat.

Not even fishing with the boys and taking your dolls' clothes to wash in the stream by the rocks while the other little girls were washing their blouses and their mothers' tortilla cloths? Or how cold the river water was? Or its lovely slate color? Its endless churning we could hear in the night even where we lived almost a mile above it?

"Those wakes sometimes got pretty wild," Maryanne said. "They started as soon as the person died and went on all night long. Many toasts down the hatch, many tears. And the deceased were supposed to be in the ground by dark the following day—so they could ride with the sun down into the land of the dead."

"Who said that, Mother?" Helen was holding her open pocketbook out toward the sun while she searched in the bottom for her keys.

"The curers, the people who teach people their prayers." It didn't matter if Helen wasn't amused. Maryanne continued, "Usually because of the drinking they'd be late starting for the cemetery. But even in the get-up-and-go and the hurrying, they always stopped and waited outside the dead person's door because it was the duty of the widow or the widower to announce there and then who she--or he--hoped to marry next."

Maryanne understood how the requirement re-enforced the idea that the heterosexual couple is the stable, basic social unit peasant communities stand upon. But having to declare so soon and under such duress also seemed strangely cruel for people who honored human feeling as much as they did in Manantiales. Lucky such declarations weren't required on the North Shore. With the crises no longer rolling in on her and no Giles to care for, Maryanne's life--daily life, surface life--had grown suddenly peaceful, pleasingly so. By chance she was on sabbatical for the whole year, and nothing especially pressing lay ahead in terms of commitments.

"What's this about, Mom? You're not contemplating marrying again so soon, I hope."

"Oh no. But you know, when I go down to the village for errands now, I can <u>feel</u> the men my own age (and the older ones too), they do have their eye out for me. In places like the drugstore where the aisles are narrow, they even edge away a little."

Helen laughed once, opened her van door and slid in. "Afraid you'll pounce?"

"Something like that. Wouldn't it be easier on everybody if <u>I'd</u> been forced to declare my intentions already?"

Helen was half in the seat, key in the ignition, but with her left boot still out planted in the snow. "Mom, what's happening with Dad's ashes?" She made herself sound enormously tired.

"I have them. They've been here a while."

"Oh, OK. You just hadn't said anything."

"Maybe it's time to put them up and start flicking our butts at them."

Helen laughed again, almost a real one this time, and then her eyes seemed to tear up a little. Maybe the cold, the wind. She tucked her foot in and closed the door, fastened her seat belt, started up, and pushed the button to roll down her window part way. "You take care, Mom. OK?" she said, her leather-gloved hand up shielding her eyes from the brightness.

⅋

Deep down the children's bickering and their suspicions about her going back to Mexico did not touch Maryanne that much. The only real threat to the new calm she had come into was that the terrain also seemed to contain crevasses, dead, weightless spaces she fell into sometimes with no warning. Absence. Nowhere. Though bewildering, disconcerting, the experience wasn't exactly frightening. She could continue, maintain, do as required. It happened once in the car on Sheridan while she was driving into the city to take Junior's kids on a Sunday afternoon museum and hamburger outing. She caught her breath, managed to keep going. The sensation wasn't exactly like anything in the mourning process she had read about. Perhaps her imagination was mounting an experiment, an attempt to get to wherever it was Giles had gone. Fifteen minutes following that episode, she passed a gold-domed Polish

Catholic church. The after-mass crowd was coming down the steps in overcoats, already old people helping shaky even-older people with canes or walkers. Maryanne found herself momentarily wishing she belonged to that congregation.

Giles had had no funeral, only a Saturday afternoon gathering at the house on Prairie Avenue. Maryanne conferred with the children, but they were even less well-organized than she was in that moment and none of them seemed to care what form their father's sendoff took. In the event, Maryanne's male colleagues soon drifted into the den to watch football and politic each other about a new senior position Anthro was angling after. The head of the department had prepared a eulogy, so everyone was herded back into the living room and the hall while he read a long list of Giles's accomplishments. Maryanne found herself wondering what there would have been to say if Giles hadn't written so much and been president of the triple-A for a year. According to these people apparently not much.

Funny, the tribe of anthropologists: studying other people's rituals but never quite developing satisfying ones of their own. The five-day annual orgy of paper-giving, horse-trading, and boozy hiya-hiyas with old friends in the halls of some huge major-city hotel they called "The Meetings" was hardly an original contribution to festivology.

"Mom?" It was Junior on the phone. From his office, she could tell, since he always talked fast when he was there, as though he was billing her at his firm's hefty rate. "I've been thinking. About Chiapas? Why not wait and go with Rennie when she goes down there in January?"

How did Junior know <u>that</u> plan? Maryanne had thought Helen had enlisted both of her sisters in her guerilla action against their brother. So did Junior and Rennie communicate behind Helen's back? Possible. As children, only boy and youngest girl had been frequent allies.

Of the four, Rennie was the slowest to get her life going. She had dawdled through an MFA in studio art and now finally at almost 30 had one year of teaching third grade under her belt. But had decided she <u>must</u> learn Spanish--perfectly, of course, she <u>was</u> her father's child--before taking on another classroom. Her plan to leave for language school either in Oaxaca or La Antigua in Guatemala was put on hold by Giles's illness. Currently it seemed stalled out due to vagaries in Rennie's relationship with her boyfriend Eric. A substitute in Chicago city schools, Eric was big, a large mop of dense dark curls and outsized, well-defined hands he waved about a lot when he was expounding. He was given to announcing 'Well, that's a plan!' seemingly as a cover for the fact that he, like Rennie, was never very sure of what he was doing next. Maryanne thought perhaps it was their--what would the nice word be?--their <u>spontaneity</u> which bound Eric and Rennie to one another.

Trying to remain the dutiful mom, Maryanne set up a meeting with Rennie--but only after she'd gone down to the village and picked up her airline tickets. Rennie chose the Art Institute for lunch, which required Maryanne's going down to the city. A little anxious about driving when she was alone in the car, she arrived quite early and got to spend nearly an hour looking at pictures. Rennie was late, so Maryanne went ahead and got a table in the café.

"*Madame*?" Someone behind her was addressing Maryanne in French.

It was a whole gaggle of tourists, eight of them, saying they hadn't been able to find the Joseph Cornells. Could she help? Had the museum moved the boxes? Apparently not, according to the map of the building they spread out before her. Maryanne did the best she could, though her French was old and classroom only and probably sounded weirdly like Spanish to the native speakers. Getting up to leave, the tourists thanked her profusely, one after the other. Maryanne was amused they had chosen her. Was it because she kept her hair short and shaped and because she "dressed," suits, stockings, small earrings? (Once at the meetings a southern friend surveyed a crowded hotel cocktail lounge crowd, the bolo ties with the paperweight-size turquoise clasps, the dashikis, the floor-sweeping batik skirts and the jangling copper flatware necklaces, and then said to Maryanne, "Honey, I believe you are the only anthropologist of our generation who doesn't come to these things all ethnic.")

Rennie showed up breathless and apologetic, ears and nose bright red. No hat, no gloves, but Maryanne didn't say anything. The girl ordered a bagel with lox and soup. She said she was tending now toward Oaxaca, a home-stay and a Spanish immersion course starting in January.

And Guatemala?

The peace there Rennie deemed too fragile. She and Eric had been on the Internet. "Mother," she said sternly, "there are still abductions and abuses going on down there. You know that, don't you?"

"There are," Maryanne said. "I do know. In Guatemala. I'm going to Chiapas, dear. Saturday, in fact."

"And you don't worry about the Zapatistas?"

"Not since the Mexican Army has pulled back. Not at all, in fact."

"Eric says that Chiapas used to be a part of Guatemala."

Maryanne nodded. "Up until a hundred and seventy-five years ago it was."

Then for several minutes Rennie skirted on about how <u>rocky</u> things were right now with Eric. Sometimes he wanted an open relationship—whatever in hell <u>that</u> meant--sometimes he seemed to think they should get married as soon as they got to Mexico.

Her ginger pumpkin soup arrived, then the bagel. Rennie slurped, then buttered, spread cream cheese, laid two thin pink strips of salmon in an 'x' across the white surface. She stopped and contemplated her mother's face.

"You know why I really admire you? Because at bottom you're a quite selfish person, aren't you, Mom? You pretend, but you never really cared about Dad and you don't really care about any of us either, do you? Self-absorbed, self-protected. That's Dr. Messer's opinion."

Rennie's psychiatrist. Maryanne and Giles—now Maryanne alone—paid his bill every month. Well. So. Now that Rennie was going to come into a little money, maybe that should change. Maryanne doubted the doctor had said any such thing, of course. She wanted to mention 'self-absorbed' and 'self-protected' might be terms you'd think of when describing her daughters, especially her darling little Rennie, but didn't.

"...or at least not enough."

"Not enough what, dear?" The 'dear' slipped out from habit. She hadn't meant it, and in the context it sounded somehow mean.

"Care. Of course you cared <u>for</u> us, I mean you fed us and all--"

Folded your underwear, matched your socks and put 'em away in the drawer, Maryanne thought.

Then for a moment she had the sensation she was falling through a trapdoor, hard landing in another one of those empty, Giles-less places. And not because of Rennie's clichés. It did not seem these territories opened up <u>because</u> of anything, much less on any schedule. The falling sensation ended and she checked herself and was OK. More or less. She waited, searching her daughter's frowning, anxious face to see was there to be more bottled venom forthcoming. Hurtful as the charge was, Maryanne wasn't about to take it up or argue back. Briefly she tried to imagine how badly Rennie must be feeling at the moment, but it was hard to do. Instead, she found herself thinking of earlier tears. *The tears that hard-to-manage crinkle of Rennie's hair had brought on when Rennie just wanted to be a conventional little Logan Elementary 4th grade doll baby, and how smart it looked now as a kind of right-on honky woman's combination halo and afro.*

The really worrisome thing was that these attacks, social suicide missions or whatever they were, seemed to be becoming regular features of Rennie's act. Maryanne even believed if she were just a little more observant she might be able to figure when the girl was about to strike. Hadn't it been there in her determined stride this afternoon as she entered the restaurant, clearly bent on something? Maryanne thought of World War II pictures where the deckhands look up and see the little speck in the sky far out over the vast Pacific and hear distantly the straining of the kamikaze's faltering, whiny engine. Was Rennie angling to cut herself off from everyone who cared about her through hatefulness? Live as some kind of batty dirty apartment hermit?

Eric—at least the existence of Eric in Rennie's life— suddenly seemed to have more importance than Maryanne had ever given it. Then a stab. What if the girl picked at Eric too? He didn't seem a man of vast patience. What then?

But now, in the moment, the girl herself appeared entirely calm, as though nothing had happened, chomping and chewing the last of the bagel, leaning forward head almost to bowl to spoon in the rest of her soup.

At the open pantry door behind Rennie's big frizzy golden mass a dishwasher, a skinny Latino, had paused with an unlit cigarette in his lips, head cocked toward the radio on the shelf above him. It was a song Maryanne knew. The restaurant had nearly cleared out and in the silence she could hear the tenor singing, ¿Cuantas veces tendré que volver? 'How many times will I have to return?' Though arguably not at the same level of artistry, the song was simple and persuasive in the style of an aria by Verdi or Puccini or at least a Nino Rota, easy, memorable.

How many times? Maryanne thought. *Once should do it.*

Thinking of the tickets to Mexico City and then on to Tuxtla sticking out of her passport case snug in the drawer of her dresser at home seemed to represent a kind of security otherwise missing from her current life.

ᠸᠵ

"Before there were anthropologists in San Cristóbal...."

The phrase had long been employed by the foreigners and even some of the local intellectuals to connote a distant, mystic, improbable past, an era no living being could possibly remember anymore. But in fact before there were anthropologists in San Cristóbal there had been Lois Shapiro and Janice Metz, artists from New York who arrived in the early fifties. Maryanne did not meet them when she first arrived in Chiapas because she and Giles thought it their duty to get to Manantiales right away and stay out there as much as possible. In the eighteen months of their first fieldwork, Maryanne made only two trips down to town. The first time she went to confirm with a physician what she was already sure of, that she was pregnant. But then she was undecided--thinking she <u>should</u> try to deliver in the field, get the women to help her, have that experience, learn how it was done in Manantiales--and so waited too long and nearly gave birth to Helen in a cave off the trail halfway to town in the middle of a terrible rainstorm. Giles and the Mayan man accompanying them got her to San Cristóbal the next morning soon after dawn. And there, as though by magic, were Lois and

Janice to take Maryanne to the one local doctor they trusted in those days. Helen was delivered that afternoon. Then for a week Lois and Janice fed and tended Giles, who became all fussy and inefficient in the face of becoming a father. Afterward, though the two couples sometimes didn't see one another for years on end, their friendship formed in a time of emergency always had about it the quality of happy though casual urgency.

Lois's last ten years were marked with bad health, suffering, and expensive crises, air ambulances to Houston and so forth, Janice on constant alert. Lois lived to be 88. Janice was now at that age and, aside from arthritis and the pain of solitude, seemed in good shape. On their first visit, in the pleasure of seeing Janice again and catching up Maryanne hardly even took account of Lois's absence. But then the following evening she went by to walk Janice down the hill to a party some of the other long-timers were having. And in the pause while the old girl was out getting her coat, Maryanne noticed how the pictures in the ladies' living room had been rearranged. Before, the two women had always displayed their own work fairly equally. Now Janice had removed her own black and white photographs and filled the large creamy walls with Lois's bright abstractions. Self-abnegation? Or was it the way Janice had discovered to deal with the same empty-pit feeling Maryanne was experiencing? In her own case, she found it hard to imagine she would be comforted by surrounding herself with more of Giles's things. For years they had been like two nations in a border dispute, Giles pushing the lines of his stuff forward across their common territory whenever Maryanne wasn't vigilant.

On the way down the cold corridor to the front door, hovering a little so she could help if her older friend needed it, Maryanne couldn't avoid seeing how thin, bony even, Janice had become in the flanks. In the past, she had always been as she said herself a "hippy woman," dieting off and on whenever she had trouble pulling on her slacks.

A memory: Janice in 1957 or 58. Most mornings you would find her down in the busy old market by the jail. Though her Spanish was still fairly stumbling, Janice made friends with many of the vendors, women especially, both Indians and Spanish-speaking ladinas. Borrowing one of their little chairs she would sit beside their displays and pull out and ready her Rolleiflex. Then wait. Once Maryanne was idly regarding a heap of undyed sheep's wool when one hank at the edge suddenly moved, as though it meant to escape. That gave Maryanne a start, then a laugh. Not wool, of course, but Janice's already-gray head. People in the market who figured out what the gringa was up to were seldom affronted, though sometimes Indian men would assume the photographs of themselves or their wives or children must be for sale, or that they should be paid for them the way outsiders were sometimes forced to pay to take their photographs at home in the municipios.

At the glass-paned doors into the room that had been Lois's studio and bedroom, Janice halted and leaned on her cane. "I can't bring myself to do anything about her clothes," she confided to Maryanne.

"What <u>should</u> you do?"

"Give them away or throw them away or <u>something</u>, shouldn't I?"

"I don't see why you have to. Wait until you feel right about it."

"Well when's that going to be?" Janice demanded. "I don't have all the time in the world myself anymore, you know."

Maryanne laughed. "I haven't touched Giles's things yet either."

This was only technically true. Though she hadn't herself gotten into his possessions, at Thanksgiving she made Junior and his oldest son go through their father/grandfather's wardrobe to see what they wanted. But they turned out to be picky, man <u>and</u> boy, took a necktie here, a pair of pajamas there, a couple of Giles's worn Pendleton shirts. Maryanne had somehow thought they would cart away garbage bags full of clothes and leave her drawers and closets to reorganize and fill for herself.

She had Janice about ready to go out the front door when Lola appeared, mewing and rubbing up against her mistress's leg, and Janice insisted on going back to lock her in. There were two household cats, Lola and Buster, both entirely black but distinguishable by size—Buster the male much bigger than Lola the female—and by attitude. As the only man on the place, Buster exerted himself primarily in his leap up onto the kitchen sink and from there to the top of a bookcase where he spent most of his time sleeping. Lola was an explorer and inveterate hunter, allowed out for long periods though Janice insisted she be confined to the sala at night. Buster showed affection in only the laziest way, but although indifferent to others Lola spent hours and hours asleep pushed up against Janice's thigh on the couch, occasionally petted and scratched around the ears.

Once they were on the street, Janice moved along slowly but earnestly, firmly taking Maryanne's hand where the cobbles were especially uneven, steadying herself, stopping to rest. She breathed in great gulps of the cold air and let it out in what sounded like long sighs. Once called Ciudad Real, for its first three centuries San Cristóbal had been the seat of colonial government for a large region. Many of the sidewalks were a foot or more above the street, supposedly to convenience gentlemen mounting horses and ladies getting into conveyances. In the rainy season the high *banquetas* also served to keep the heavy torrents of water moving downhill toward the river. Janice had learned to avoid the sidewalks and walk mostly in the narrow street, stopping and turning her back to cars and taxis when they came whizzing out of nowhere and zoomed by.

"Will you be going out to Manantiales?"

"I had hoped to."

"There's a bus every day now they say."

"A truck, yes. I was told so. But it goes in the afternoon and doesn't come back until the morning," Maryanne said. "I would imagine I could find someone still alive who'd remember me and let me stay over, but--"

"You don't want to risk it."

"Getting stuck. No."

Now for some reason Janice wanted to proceed up on the banqueta. She bumped her cane along until she came to a place where the sidewalk paving dipped lower a ways. "Here," she said, staking her cane. "This is one of the places I could get Lois up."

The way of the one left behind, what Maryanne was just learning. Already she too insisted on noting to herself ordinary little places that for one reason or another had Giles attached to them. Things too. A piece of his soap turning to brown jelly in a dish in the bathroom at Prairie Avenue, a pair of tennis shoes with the laces still tied together from the last time he went to the gym.

Janice continued on resolutely, apparently not aware of Maryanne stumbling along behind touching her eyes with a Kleenex and trying to catch up.

Below them now came into view the whole bowl of the San Cristóbal valley, the blacker silhouettes of mountains low against the huge dark but starry sky, the city twinkling—shimmering, actually—in the clear night air, brighter by an order of magnitude than Maryanne's memory of it. In their first articles forty year ago she and Giles referred to it only as a town. San Cristóbal claimed to 25,000 inhabitants then, but people from the municipal building told them there were really only 17,000 and the number was still shrinking. Though the tortuously winding section of the Pan American Highway that brought access to the outside world up to San Cristóbal was finally completed, young people used the new road to get away—those with money to get an education, those without to escape the class-bound provinciality and boredom of the place. But by the cusp of the 21st century, only three weeks ahead now, the human tide in San

Cristóbal was long reversed. Nowadays, Maryanne had been told, they under-estimated the population, said actually to be well over 300,000, because there was no city water or sewage for a third of the households. There had been a middle-class migration from Mexico City after the earthquake there in 1985, which dramatically increased the number of restaurants and gift shops in "SanCris" as people now called it, and lately new university campuses and several study centers which offered advanced degrees. But the really significant growth was in the number of indigenous residents, protestant converts considered turncoats in their home communities or families without land forced here to scratch out a living however they could. These new people, only recently converted to ladino clothing and still Maya-speakers, lived mostly outside the old grid of streets along the *periférico* or circle road that girded the city. At night the improvised sprawls of their colonias irregularly sloshed electric light up the sides of the mountains, in some places nearly to the top.

The party was at the home of Maryanne's and Janice's old friend Petra Hobbs and Petra's new husband, a slim, tall Italian literary fellow named Sandro. Petra never went long without a partner. Sandro was Number Three, or maybe it was Four, acquired after the last one had his heart attack. A year or so before Petra gave up her distinguished professorship at Brandeis, she bought a 150-year-old house on a busy street in downtown San Cristóbal and began fixing it up whenever she and Sandro were free to come down. (Sandro seemed eternally free. It was not clear exactly what he did.) The place had enormous great beamed ceilings, big columns along the corridor, a fountain in the patio with some sort of statue that spouted a little burbling trickle of water. Fireplace in the living room, another in the connected dining room, modern-enough kitchen. An outscale grandeur, especially for Petra, who was short and round, an engine of energy, and a lifelong socialist.

It took Maryanne only a few minutes to realize the idea of the return had hardly been uniquely hers. Nearly every living gringo anthropologist she knew who had ever worked in Chiapas seemed to be at the party. And the dead? Who knew how many of <u>those shades</u> might not be lurking up the chimney or making their phantom passes at the table with the tamales and the booze? Among the still-here of her own generation, about half now appeared to be on the wagon and the other half needed to think about getting aboard pronto. The years helped them to get drunk quicker and on less, but had not dimmed their ardor for loose talk.

Some of the move to come back had to do with the Zapatista uprising in 1994. Called upon to comment on the masked Indian men and women and their exotic blue-eyed commander Marcos by reporters from their local paper or to write a how-did-this-happen piece for one of the journals, the anthropologists had opined as required, but the experience made many of them also realize how short they were on real data. What <u>had</u> changed so in Chiapas since their day that another Maya revolt would brew up? So, retired as most of them were by now, and free, they came to find out.

And, it seemed, to purchase real estate. Petra wasn't the only one. Among the survivors, the few who hadn't bought houses in town yet were a bit touchy or defensive about it, like people who have turned down the chance to invest in a successful Broadway show. Maryanne talked with a woman she had known 40 years but whose name didn't come immediately to mind. The woman had on beautiful gold filigree earrings and sported a large moonstone set in silver on her chest. In a conspiratorial way she leaned toward Maryanne and said, "Personally, I don't see what they see in this place anymore."

"But you're here too, aren't you?"

"Oh yes, I come still, can't stay away. But well, you know—"

"I do? Know what?"

"Well, the mist has gone off the mountains, if you know what I mean--"

Someone was tapping Maryanne on the shoulder, so she just smiled and turned to include the tapper in the conversation. Another old friend, also her own age, thinned out and with his sparse gray hair pulled back into a ratty little ponytail. He wanted to give her a big enveloping hug, so Maryanne let him.

About the mists... Filigree Earrings couldn't mean literally, could she? Still plenty of cloud spewing over the mountain crests in first sunlight, plenty of blankets of white obscuring the road ahead, wisping through the treetops....

Ponytail, whose name Maryanne <u>did</u> with some effort pull up--Evan Richards he was—was saying, "All you have to do to see what's happened is go just once to the market. San Cristóbal has become an indigenous city. Everyone senses it, but the ladinos certainly aren't going to admit that's what's happened, and the Indians aren't ready to proclaim themselves quite yet. All those people displaced from their municipios over the years living up in La Hormiga and the other places like it? And then the Zapatistas come along and show the world how easy it would be to take control by force instead of by creeping demographics! <u>That</u> gave people courage you can be sure."

A plump young woman with her hair in a large, loose chignon, once a graduate student of Petra's, mentioned that she had been working out at ECOSUR, the research campus at the edge of the San Cristóbal valley, right before the Zapatistas arrived. "And you know, the Army post is close nearby. We'd pass it when we went on hikes to the Arcotete or up into the hills. So end of '93 I was in New York to see my family and New Year's Day I get a call from my friends all excited because CNN is saying masked rebels toting rifles have overrun the military stronghold outside SanCris. And I'm thinking 'stronghold'? With the gate open all the time and especially on a holiday with everybody on leave and no soldiers much around? Yeah, I'd guess three or four guys with guns could probably stroll right in and take over that place no problem."

Maryanne laughed. Evan Richards was nodding and agreeing, but Filigree Earrings seemed distracted, peering down into her cup, looking with what seemed like longing and doubt together toward the drink table. A moment later she wandered away.

Petra had had two large windows installed, one in the living room, the matching one in the dining room, to give views out into her patio, a lush space planted in elephant ear, cacti and palms and small trees with bromeliads brought up from the jungle depending from the crotches of some branches. Though it was too dark to see out now, Petra and Janice were going back and forth, followed by willowy Sandro, assaying one and then the other of the big black rectangles. Janice's partner Lois had spent years making dazzling translucent abstract panels which needed to be lit from behind to get the full effect of their color. She built some panels into light boxes so they could sit on mantels or be free-standing in a gallery or a home, but others were in simple wood frames and required hanging in windows. Janice had been more or less offhand with Maryanne when she mentioned Petra and her new husband were thinking about buying two or three of the "transglows," which was Lois's not-entirely-right name for them. But now Janice trucked back and forth, staking her cane and staking it again, her mouth fixed a little grim in heavy concentration. If some of Lois's bigger pieces were going to come to reside here, how they were placed was serious business for her.

The younger people at the party were funny, condescending while thinking they were being oh-so-polite. They wanted 'desperately' (Maryanne heard the word twice in an hour) to learn how things were 'back then' 'in your time.' But when you made the mistake of launching into any description of 'then,' they would touch your arm and smile and flee in the middle of your sentence.

Sandro the husband seemed to feel being the host meant keeping everyone's glass or ceramic cup filled. He had expensive tequilas from the north laid out, but among the old-timers who were still drinking most stuck with Bacardi. Petra's big ball of strawberry hair (these days at least touched some by the bottle) made her look in a way as though she, rather than Maryanne, should be Rennie's mom. The ball bobbed up and down as she expounded, pleasantly sloshed, to several of the youngers. "Of course in the beginning we never had a method. My advisor--" and here she mentioned a man many in the room thought of more as a university building than a person "--told me to take my flashlight and my flea powder and not to sleep with married men in my village because I would need the women as allies. And that was it, all he wrote!"

In the little group surrounding Petra was a tall, plump, flushed fellow with a short brown and gray beard who Maryanne couldn't exactly place. He had billed himself to her earlier as 'more of a historian actually' than an anthropologist. Almost 60, about to early retire from the University of Florida, she thought he had said. Turning to her now he asked, "Is that how you remember it, Mrs. Fort?"

As the others moved on to other things, regrouping, Maryanne considered. "No. I always thought Giles and I pretty much did know what we were doing. We were young but full of curiosity, wonder really, and we didn't doubt ourselves or the enterprise of ethnography all the time as the current generation of students are persuaded they should. That was what fieldwork seemed to be about. Following your instincts. Using your head."

"But then you were like Petra. It was intuition you let guide you."

"I suppose. Or maybe expedience or chance."

"Is there an example?"

She thought a moment. "The second time we lived in Manantiales. I had two children by then and they were claiming they couldn't go outside because the Indian kids were throwing stones at the house we'd rented. And they <u>were</u> throwing stones, although more to get the little gringos' attention than in actual hostility I thought. So I invited everybody in to draw pictures at our work table and they all became friends. And as a result, I ended up with a collection of over 800 Mayan children's drawings."

"Which led to your 'Revealed Content in Imaginative Work of Highland Maya Pre-adolescents.' Lovely piece of work."

Maryanne laughed. "Today I wouldn't have put such a stodgy title to it." She was both pleased and put off by the more-of-a-historian's ability to recite so readily from her CV. His name was Rufus Bright. Gay, she had the feeling. Hadn't a lover been mentioned, or a 'partner' with no sex attached?

"I've always found your writing evokes more than Giles's ever did. More thought in it too."

Was Mr. Bright looking to make points? And why was he calling a man he'd never met by his first name?

Maryanne was silent. She gazed off over Rufus's shoulder, then said, "I still have all those drawings somewhere."

In the double garage out on the alley at home. Giles had laid sheets of plywood across the rafters and together they lifted boxes and boxes of old field notes and text up there, covered them with sheets of opaque plastic, folded and taped down the corners.

What irked her really was not this Bright's chumminess or even his finding Giles's work wanting. It was an older business. Despite Giles's sole credit on <u>Cornucopia</u>, she had imagined readers would understand how much the work had been done by both of them. The gender stuff, the material on child-rearing and child development and on the lives of women couldn't have been gathered by a man. For many years before professional meetings she and Giles would toss a coin to decide which one would give their paper. Maryanne always used "we" when talking about their work. And for many years at least in her presence Giles did the same. When the shift came, Maryanne was slow to pick up on it. With children and doing what she could to help Giles secure good jobs, she lagged almost a decade behind him in getting her degree. One of the venerables on her committee passed away and a new member had to be appointed. In the last 15 minutes of Maryanne's oral exams--she was already breathing easier and wondering how wet Cecile would be when she retrieved her from the friend waiting outside--some sandy-haired whippersnapper opined that her dissertation would make a "fine addition to Giles's original ethnography." She found herself thinking *Just a minute, young man, just a damn minute!* while at the same time reminding herself she was a grad student still and this <u>kid</u> had some sway over her. Worse, the other men ranged around the table, their backs to the windows so Maryanne couldn't even see their familiar faces, had begun to nod and agree.

The conversation with Bright had moved on, but maybe because she had had a couple of drinks, Maryanne wasn't quite sure where it had gone. She found herself defending the time-honored practice of sending young married couples to the field together. How else would you deal with the fact that in traditional culture the spheres of men's and women's lives <u>are</u> often nearly completely separate?

Maybe time to corral Janice and leave. Everyone in the room seemed to be shouting at everyone else. Only bad behavior or lumpishness could follow.

Wanting to end on an easier note, she said to Rufus Bright, "You and your partner ever do fieldwork together?"

"Oh no," Rufus laughed. "He was in advertising." He tilted his glass up in a kind of half-toast to the heavens and then drained it. "And besides, you know as well as I do no one does fieldwork <u>per</u> <u>se</u> anymore."

Was he being ironic? Maryanne looked around. In a conspiratorial whisper she asked, "Then what are all these people doing here? <u>Per</u> <u>se</u>?"

"What Nick Bunnin says anthropologists have always done: they have sought and found a most beautiful and congenial place where they can live on the cheap."

"And what makes you different?"

"I'm back to San Cristóbal these days mainly to root around in the bishop's archive."

"So let me get this straight--" Maryanne set her glass down on the embroidered Guatemalan runner of the drinks table. "Working with human leavings called documents makes you somehow <u>better</u> than those of us who trudge along anachronistically trying to understand the living. Is that it?"

Rufus put his glass down rather precisely next to hers. "Mrs. Fort," he said, "I was really pleased to get to talk with you tonight. Whether you were aware of it or not, you and your husband helped impel me into my own life in crime or history or anthropology or whatever it is I do. I feel honored to have met up with you again after all these years and I have been <u>very</u> sad ever since I heard about Giles."

"Not to have collected the whole set?"

He peered at her, his eyes all big, and shook his head. "You don't know who I am, do you?"

"Not really."

"I was a student in Giles's project."

From the middle Sixties well into the Seventies, Giles had National Science Foundation money to bring graduate students to Mexico for a summer of training. An entirely worthwhile endeavor (at least many of the alumni of it went on to worthwhile careers), but easy on the Forts, closer to a vacation than to work. They rented a warm, window-filled house on the outskirts of San Cristóbal, Maryanne kept a garden, the children rode horses, and Giles wrote all morning, then took the project's Toyota jeep out to visit students in the municipios where they were placed. Weekends the young people were free to come into town, Giles organized a seminar session, and in the evening there was food and a marimba and the dancing sometimes went on till two or three in the morning.

Maryanne looked closer at Rufus's flushed face, the dark eyes, the doggish look his tongue peeking out between his lips gave him. "I'm sorry, I <u>don't</u> remember you."

"I came that first summer, the one you didn't. Nineteen sixty-five."

"Oh no, I always—"

But the historian was right. She <u>had</u> missed the first year. Stayed home to see her own mother through a cataract operation and to have Junior, who had to come by C-section.

"I know <u>your</u> work too then, Rufus. Very admirable." Rufus Bright. Influenced more by Murdo McCloud than by his time with Giles. Although Giles would claim him, or at least proudly mention that he had helped push Rufus in the direction of the history of Mexico and Central America.

"I think it's time for me to get out of here," said Maryanne.

"Me too. Shall I walk you?"

"No. My hotel is only a few blocks up. And I have Janice to get safely home. But thanks."

Janice, it turned out, had found someone else to help her navigate the cobbles and had already snuck away. Maryanne and not-so-young Rufus said their goodbyes and went out into the night air. It felt as though there might be frost later on. Maryanne started off in her direction. And despite her having refused his invitation, Rufus came plodding somewhat less steadily after her. The nighttime lighting in San Cristóbal had improved, but only in the center of town. Beyond the magic circle the streets remained woefully dark, which left the stars overhead nearly as big as ever. Maryanne could hear Rufus slipping and sliding behind her, and once he called out "Yow!" and she turned and saw him tilting, his long arms spread and angling up and down like a kite or a hawk in a capricious wind, before he regained balance.

At the corner she stopped and said, "If you're going to insist on this, you may as well go first."

"Like the Indians? Well, OK," he said, pushing past her, "I am the man, I guess."

"Yes," she said. Then as they were moving on, she added, "How'd you know that detail, Mr. Don't-Do-Fieldwork?"

"Oh, I did it too—fieldwork, that is--" he called back, "back in the day. Chamula, I lived in Tzajalemel."

The tall, iron-bound wooden portals of her hotel were fast shut. Maryanne had to ring the bell and wait for the *velador*. (*Lovely that the Spanish for a "candle" should survive into the two-thousands in the word for a watchman*, she thought). When the boy opened the little door cut in the righthand big one and there was light behind him, she turned to Rufus and said, "Thanks for seeing me home," and put out her hand.

Rufus took Maryanne's in his own big hands and then wouldn't quite let her go. "Remind me. How long has it been?" he asked.

"What? Since Giles died? A little over two months."

"It does get easier, you know. It will."

She retrieved her hand and jammed it in the pocket of her coat. But she didn't mean to reject him or whatever it was he was offering, so she stood there, exhaling breath forcefully in a narrowed tube as though it were cigarette smoke and watching it turn to white mist.

"I don't want to get into comparisons," Rufus said, "but I'm a widow too, you know. My Javier died a year ago."

"I'm sorry to hear that," she said. "Look, it's cold. I'm going in."

"I hope we can talk again."

"Maybe we can. Good night." She stepped inside and the velador came forward to close the door.

"We've danced together, you know." Bright was smiling broadly.

"Have we? When was that?"

"That same summer. You <u>did</u> come, briefly, for maybe ten days toward the end--"

"I—" She was going to object, but then she remembered. Once she'd seen her mother through her eye operation and had Junior, she took her month-old down to Giles's mother's near Evansville. It was Grandma Fort who said she'd be glad to watch after him if Maryanne wanted a little time in Mexico with the rest of the family. The old lady was so easy with the little guy and took such a delight in him that Maryanne had no trepidation about going.

"Was I drunk?" she asked Bright.

He laughed. "Tipsy, maybe. Why do you ask?"

"By that stage in my life unless I'd had something to drink I wasn't dancing much with anybody."

Certainly not with Giles's male grad students, she thought.

"It was entirely fun, I can promise you."

"Well good!" she said. The velador stood waiting. She felt better now about the historian than she had all evening.

Good nights were said again and the big door closed. She stood, listening to the boy shooting the bolts into place. On the ground lay a pile of ragged blankets on top of straw where the boy had been sleeping. A gray kitten poked its sleepy head out, as though, she thought, to ask the kid, *Why'd you get out of bed? And when are you coming back?*

03

The next day Maryanne returned from a little Christmas shopping at the market and was handed a note from Rufus the ethnohistorian saying he had "some perhaps good news" for her and would call again at the hotel. Maryanne was in the dining room when he showed up with a small Mexican woman in a dark suit and stockings. Rufus introduced her. Her name was Rosalie Utrillo. Rufus asked did Maryanne know her.

"I think I must," Maryanne replied, looking up, smiling. Though she didn't like being put on the spot this way, she invited them to join her. Another chair was brought and her unexpected guests sat. Maryanne regarded the other woman's small features, her dark skin, the fact she was wearing rouge as well as lipstick. Forty-five or fifty maybe, Maryanne thought. And sitting bemusedly on some secret, or maybe some story she wanted to tell.

But it was Rufus who couldn't wait. "This is Rosie Tu'ul, Maryanne," he said.

"Oh my goodness!" Maryanne's hands went to her own cheeks and without thinking she was on her feet, pulling Rosie up and to her. "Excuse me," she whispered in Spanish, meaning for not recognizing the other woman.

As she hugged Rosie she became aware of Rosie gently patting her back and pulling in deep breaths.

Rosie had been the first girl from Manantiales to get a Spanish-language education and become a primary-school teacher. She had just turned 14 when the Forts came to live in the room behind the schoolhouse. She and Maryanne quickly began to call each other 'older sister' and 'younger sister' in Tzeltal and Maryanne helped Rosie with her arithmetic. For a number of years Maryanne was able to follow Rosie's progress through the school system when she came to Mexico and by way of an irregular but warm correspondence when they were four thousand miles apart. Then, sometime after Rosie finished the equivalent of high school on a scholarship at a Catholic girls' academy in Puebla and began teaching, their communication became much more sporadic and then the thread was lost. Now as they were catching up, Maryanne remembered that the man Rosie had written she was to marry was not an Indian and that the surname she mentioned was "Utrillo." Perhaps Maryanne had forgotten these facts because she hadn't held much hope for the marriage. But apparently it had survived. Señor Utrillo was retired, Rosie still working, a supervisor now, and they too had grandchildren and lived in a neighborhood out on the edge of San Cristóbal.

Shyly, Rosie said, "Mr. Rufus told me you wanted to visit Manantiales."

"Oh yes, I do. Very much," Maryanne said.

"You'll find it's different."

"I know I will."

"Do you want to go this afternoon?"

It was already two o'clock. Wouldn't it be better to go another day? Maryanne asked.

Oh no, Rosie laughed, her husband drove like a demon. He would have them there in plenty of time to talk with people. If Maryanne wouldn't mind coming back in the dark. They had had it in mind to go out to the community today anyway.

Always better to fit into other people's plans than to insist on your own--a rule Maryanne and Giles had followed in their fieldwork. Maryanne nearly ran across the lobby and up the stairs to leave her sweater and get a coat and some things. She was so filled with emotion she thought of stopping to wash her face and calm down. But the cold water in her bathroom was so cold and the warm took so long to come up that she dropped the idea.

And besides, what was wrong with being stirred by such strong feeling? Homecoming. The return. *Less events really,* she thought, *than emotions in themselves.*

Maryanne and Rosie took a cab to Rosie's house. The Utrillos' boxy little living room was nearly filled by a clunky wood and nubbled brown upholstered sofa-and-loveseat set and a huge TV they apparently left running all the time. Souvenir weavings and Maya-motif medallions commemorating trips to Copán and Tikál on the walls. They had a maid, clearly an Indian but dressed as a ladina. The husband introduced was probably about Maryanne's own age, rotund and bald. He kept thanking her for coming, each time rubbing his hands together as though calculating the prestige value of Maryanne's visit.

Nothing, not even the toy back-strap looms on the wall, to indicate that there was an indigenous side to the life led here. Or not until Rosie came down from the bedroom in her Manantiales blouse holding her handwoven blue skirt up so she could see her feet and not trip on the steps. She handed Maryanne the red wool *faja* and asked would she help her pleat the skirt. The length of heavy dyed cotton was already sewn together in a large tube. Maryanne turned her hand flat like a paddle to measure as she gathered material so the folds would come out even and sharp as they fanned out from center, seven on each side. Then she wrapped the belt twice around Rosie's waist and tied its braided ends in a third go-around. In Manantiales, at least in the old days, while Rosie would not have finished dressing this way in front of a man, even her husband, asking the oldest woman present to make her pleats was certainly the height of good manners.

☙

Manantiales are springs, and in the village there were places
where freshets poured out of the hillsides most of the year. The
spring water was used for drinking and cooking, the river below
for washing clothes. Manantiales also had an older Mayan
name which translated as something like 'always-producing
land.' One day Giles said, "They think of this place--they trust
it to give--as though it were a cornucopia." The other reason
they called the community 'Cornucopia' in their writing had
to do with the terrain. The river ran past the village center
west to east. Thousands of years ago it had cut itself a deep
white gash in the limestone of the mountain to the south. On
the Manantiales side of it was a large cupped valley where the
majority of the people had their houses and their cornfields. The
pine forests and the steep mountains behind them to the north
were home to the ancestral Father/Mothers, the deities prayed
to and propitiated with chickens and candles, skyrockets and
incense and liquor. Because of the valley's orientation, sunrise
and sunset both took place out of sight of most of the dwellings.
Early on Maryanne and Giles recognized this as a material cause
of a mysterious expectancy they felt so often when they were in
Manantiales. Daybreak and sundown were both occasions for
spectacular displays of dense color, but the source of the effect
was forever off-stage, the miracle--so to speak--taking place
beyond the mouth of the horn of plenty.

Though she had herself steeled for major changes after
twenty years, what Maryanne found at first left her giddy and

a little confused. Ploughing along in Señor Utrillo's big white SUV the trip in to the village took nearly an hour less than what she had been told. Though the paved road generally followed the old dirt one (and much of the horse or mule path of <u>her</u> day), they went whizzing along at such speed that she nearly missed many of her remembered landmarks. They were a hundred yards beyond what she <u>thought</u> must be the cave or limestone overhang where she had nearly delivered Helen when she realized what she had just seen, a boarded-up military checkpoint and a three-tier observation tower, abandoned and going to rust.

"I didn't know the Army had been here," Maryanne said to Rosie.

Señor Utrillo said, "The Army was everywhere after the Zapatistas came, Señora."

Maryanne knew the village was said to have supported the guerillas. "Were there arrests?"

Silence. Then Rosie said, "Some people went to jail. When they were released they moved away."

Silence again.

They reached Manantiales just after four. Right before the road broadened out the military had put in a more elaborate installation. There was a metal guard gate, raised for the time being, and a little house, and back fifty feet a larger building with a yard enclosed behind chain-link fencing. The Army had its own basketball court and three young soldiers in fatigues and t-shirts were out shooting baskets. A benign-enough scene, but Maryanne noted Rosie and Sr. Utrillo acted as though the soldiers weren't there until the men stopped and waved, and then they waved back briefly.

What was it Rufus Bright said just today? She hadn't been listening carefully. That his policy in the current period was whether they were on duty or not you nodded pleasantly to soldiers and stayed out of their way if possible. When someone came toward him with a video camera at any of the pro-Zapatista rallies in front of the cathedral, he turned and walked in the other direction. Foreigners are prohibited from engaging in political activity in Mexico. Maryanne knew that, and also that what constitutes 'political activity' is defined at will by the authorities. Rufus claimed several gringos he knew had their passports confiscated just for attending demonstrations and were escorted to the Texas border where they were given their documents back and told not to attempt to re-enter the country anytime soon.

"Do the people support the Zapatistas?"

Silence. Wrong question. Rosie looked out the window, finally said softly, "Some of them do, I think."

The village now had a "downtown," if you wanted to call it that. Manantiales had never been grand enough to have its own church, but it did have an *ermita,* an hermitage or shrine, a white chapel decorated like a psychedelic wedding cake in low-relief painted plaster, maroon and yellow flowers and butterflies and symbols in rows up and down its façade, scales, a scourge, a ladder, a rooster, a cluster of stars, the moon. The Ermita was the home of Manantiales' precious wooden saints and grand, blue- and silver-decorated crosses, which were treated as though they too, like the saints, were living beings. A new plaza had been laid out before the chapel since Maryanne's day. Now unweeded, neglected-looking. On the far side where there had been only one store, there were now a couple of them and a cantina with metal tables out front. A scratchy-picture black-and-white television blared away and provided some illumination of the dark interior. The school building had doubled in size, the room she and Giles had lived in first was now the state government agent's office and contained a telephone. Maryanne kept reaching into her bag, thinking she should make notes. But in her haste she hadn't even brought along paper, much less a camera.

One thing that hadn't changed: The kids stared at her as their parents—or more likely their grandparents--had. They would already be trained not to look so openly at a ladino, but probably nobody would have thought to warn them about gringos.

Rosie was funny. She seemed not to have forgotten a word of her own Tzeltal, but often she used the Spanish term when there was a perfectly good Mayan one available. On the ride in she informed Maryanne that in San Cristóbal she still made her own tortillas and didn't eat with a fork. Yet despite the pleated skirt and the little plastic slippers just like any other Manantiales woman's, she moved now authoritatively, brusquely. When she laughed she forgot to cover her mouth. And she ruffled the little boys' hair and kept turning their chins up so she could inspect them, very much the ladina school lady.

Maryanne knew Rosie's father had died, and had been hesitant to ask about Losha, her mother. But Rosie brought up the subject, taking it as a matter of course that Maryanne would want to go up to the top of the valley to see the old lady. Sr. Utrillo stayed behind to have a beer with the *agente* and, as he noted, keep an eye on his vehicle.

The two women climbed the hill in silence. Where the pine woods began, they paused to get their breath and gaze back down the way they had come. Maryanne experienced again that thumping in her heart which could be attributed to exertion or altitude but which she knew to be something else as well. You couldn't hear the TV from the cantina anymore, or see the silvery wires that brought in the electricity and the telephone. The steep thatched old-time roofs were gone forever, replaced with tile or corrugated tin, but otherwise, at least from up here, Manantiales looked much more as it did in her memory. A light blue haze of wood smoke lay over the valley.

"Do you remember what your father would say?"

Rosie laughed. "My father talked a great deal, you know."

"He told me once that for him to leave Manantiales in the morning or in the daytime was fine, but once the evening fires were started and you could see light coming from people's houses, it made him sad--it 'tore at him' was the way he said it-- to have to go away from home then."

Rosie nodded. Then she got a merry look in her eyes. "Maybe that's why when he had to go out at night he always flew."

Both of Rosie's parents had been curers, powerful and respected ones. As they got older, however, suspicion grew in the community that for the money they would also light black candles for you. Hence Rosie's joke, since any witch with even a modicum of magic was supposed to have mastered the techniques of night flying. Maryanne didn't know the whole story, but she suspected the reason Losha and Rosie's father had left their valley property to their other children and moved up here was to get out of the public eye, become a little passed over, forgotten. At the same time, living more in the mountains reaffirmed their connection with the ancestors who dwelled there—spirits more beneficent than harmful in people's image of them.

Her mother had been ill, Rosie told Maryanne, but when they appeared at her doorway and asked without peering in was she home, a crackly old voice came back, "I am home! Marta, open up there!" A young girl swung the wooden door open and in the gloom they could make out the old lady struggling up from a bed in the back corner. She came tottering forth to greet them with a kind of urgency, as though they might suddenly go away again.

Losha had never learned any Spanish and now she had lost most of her teeth. But for some reason—because they had known one another so long? because there were little set speeches they could employ? because Losha's rubbery, mobile face telegraphed emotion so easily?--Maryanne had no trouble understanding her Tzeltal. They sat on little stools and Marta, a granddaughter who stayed with the old lady, began building up the fire to boil water for coffee. Losha cried and sniffed and wiped her eyes on her sleeve, blaming her tears on the smoke. When the fire licked up and the smoke cleared off, Maryanne dabbed her own eyes on her shirt cuff and said in Tzeltal, "Not me, my tears are for seeing you, my mother, to see you are still alive and well."

The remembered formula started them all sniffling, even the young girl, and laughing at themselves at the same time. After the "coffee" made of brown semi-refined sugar and some sweet rolls Rosie had brought from San Cristóbal, she got out a number of plastic bottles and began to instruct her mother about how many of each pill to take. Vitamins. Losha felt each bottle, then would send little Marta over to put it on the small carnation-decorated altar in the corner.

During the pill discussion Maryanne had time to get her Timex unstrapped from her wrist and dropped into her bag. Once the vitamins were all put away, she took the watch out and presented it to Rosie's mom as her gift. The old lady held it lightly in both hands, then put it up to her ear.

"Tell her it's electric, it doesn't make any sounds," Maryanne said to Rosie in Spanish.

As Losha was thanking her, Maryanne looked frankly into her cloudy eyes and made sure. Losha had gone blind, or nearly so, probably from cataracts.

Maryanne delivered the news about Giles, but it did not seem to have much effect on either Rosie or her mother. They must have surmised it from Maryanne's coming back alone.

And in the moment--frankly, in her happiness--Giles's death had somehow lost some of its import for Maryanne as well.

The old woman said something Maryanne didn't quite catch. Rosie translated: "She says your husband liked to come up here with my father when he was learning his prayers. Do you want to go there now?"

Maryanne didn't know exactly where 'there' might be. But it was clear from Losha's upturned face that she was supposed to say yes, so she did.

They left the house and fell naturally into a little procession, Marta carrying coals from the fire in a clay incense pot, then Maryanne, and then Rosie with her mother, Losha with her chin in the air as though she was the actual navigator. It was getting toward dark, and down by the river evening mist had drifted in and mixed with the supper-fire smoke. The "town" became just a couple of electric lights floating like baubles in batting of a deep blue going to purple.

After five minutes or so tramping through the pine and oak they came to a waist-high altar built up of limestone and loosely-poured cement with blue wooden crosses festooned with maroon and green bromeliads standing behind it. There were fresh pine needles strewn thickly on the ground. Rosie's mother lit a candle and dropped wax and one by one placed four candles in an even row on the altar surface. A feat for a person working largely by touch. Then she set chunks of sweet copal sizzling in the incensor and waved it about to encourage the resin to give off smoke. (In Tzeltal, Maryanne suddenly recalled, this motion was called "wrapping us in copal's protection.") Clinging to the altar to help herself, the old woman slowly got down on her knees in the pine needles to pray. Rosie and Maryanne and Marta kneeled beside her.

Losha sang aloud for a few minutes, invoking certain Catholic saints, several Mayan deities whose names Maryanne could recognize, and the sun and the moon, in Tzeltal called "Father" and "Dear Mother." When the old lady paused, she signaled to Marta, who brought out of a net bag a shot glass and a small bottle of clear rum stoppered with a piece of dried corncob. Losha prayed briefly over the liquor, then poured shots for each of them in turn. The intense sting of the raw liquor going down Maryanne remembered so well, and then the little bounce of warmth she had forgotten. Even the little girl was given a glass. Marta sipped and made a face as she was supposed to, and was allowed to pour the rest of hers off into another bottle.

Then Losha turned to Maryanne and asked did she have anything of her husband's to "offer up." Maryanne's heart again began to thump, for in fact at the hotel she had impulsively grabbed out of her suitcase a little box containing some of Giles's ashes and stashed it in her bag. But she had no idea how Losha might react to the contents of the box. In Manantiales there was no cremation, they always put a body in the ground. So she reached in and got her wallet and pulled out two cards, Giles's driver's license and his last business card with the university seal on it. (He had left the house the last time with no billfold, only these two pieces of identification in his pocket.) Losha lightly fingered the cards, big-jointed old fingers playing along the edges, then prayed over them a minute and put them up to the candles. The paper burned easily, the plastic suddenly, letting off a thick little spurt of bad-smelling black smoke and dropping black residue onto the altar surface.

Maryanne was remembering the Saturday afternoon gathering at their house, the men's voices from the den rising over the TV commentators' and the college band songs and the spectacular, volume-enhanced commercials. Though Giles claimed to be an agnostic, he would certainly have preferred this celebration to that one.

She laughed. *Agnostic?* In the hour before he folded up and died, Giles sought her hand and whispered, "I've always loved you, sweetheart." He gathered breath and said, "And you know, 'Whom God hath joined together—'"

Losha placed her hand on Maryanne'e thigh. Maryanne was crying freely now, but it did not matter. The old lady pushed down on her a little, using the motion to adjust her own body a bit higher, then began singing again in a more urgent way.

Maryanne felt about on the ground for her bag. Had she put in one of those little packets of Kleenex? Then she gave up the search. She had some practice at letting turbulence roll inside her when it had to, and some part of her remained still, listening intently to Losha's words and, surprisingly, given that the language of prayers was archaic, understanding almost all of them. Losha was invoking still other saints and naming holy crosses, thanking mountains and the Father-Mothers for Giles's life, and including some petitions for the protection of Maryanne and her children and for herself and the other two gathered at the altar with her. Maryanne's own named came out elongated, "Ma-a-ri-AN-na-na-AY."

By the time they got back to Losha's house, black starless night had set in. The old lady asked when Maryanne would be coming back to Manantiales again. Maryanne said she didn't know. Though she recalled in Tzeltal the question was formulaic, she went on to say she had been hoping maybe their old room behind the school would be available, but it wasn't.

"No, no," Losha said, wagging her head, chin pointed up. "But you could stay here, my daughter. We could build your bed in the other corner, and sleep together when it's really cold. There aren't so <u>many</u> fleas."

The little flea joke was also a Mayan cliché, but Rosie and Marta laughed along anyway. Maryanne then should have thanked Rosie's mother grandly and promised to come soon. But she hesitated. Giles had always been convinced that in the field it was essential to have at least a room of your own where you could get away from inquiring eyes and other people's business.

"Or my son-in-law will come," Losha persisted, "and build you your own little house next door, right by us. Then we can go gather firewood and make them heat up the sweat bath for our old bones and go in there and gossip and make mischief all night. We can have the <u>life</u> of old ladies!"

From time to time now they could hear the distant tooting of Señor Utrillo playing on his Suburban's horn. Though Losha was joking some, the grandness of her offer, her generosity, overwhelmed Maryanne. She took Losha's hand and squeezed it lightly, the proper way. "I'll try to come soon, my mother."

"Yes, come soon, my daughter, come back soon," the old lady replied.

Cʒ

Christmas in Wilmette went off peacefully that year, but in no excess of goodwill. Cecile's usually polite California-blond kids paid almost no attention to stuffed animals—a snake, a tiger, a pig—or to bright wooden panel trucks loaded with armed, bandannaed little Zapatista doll men and women their grandmother brought them from Chiapas. Rennie's Eric declared his patchwork Guatemalan vest bought in the San Cristóbal crafts market a work of art, but when he tried it on the cloth ties didn't quite come together over his big belly.

Cecile unwrapped a willow basket full of Helen's fruit jellies with little gingham cloths over the lids with never a word of thanks. The two sisters went right on chatting testily about a four-star pilgrimage to Vienna, Milan, and other opera cities Helen and her husband were taking starting the first of February.

"That's about the time I'll be going back to Mexico," Maryanne said.

Brief pause and a tiny exchange of looks between daughters.

"How long would that be for, Mother?" Cecile said.

"I've left the return open. I'm going out to Manantiales and I'm even going to try to get in a little fieldwork if that turns out to be a possibility."

Silence. Finally, Helen said, "What if something should happen to you, Mother?"

"Like what?"

More silence. So Maryanne said, "What would be the worst? That I would have a heart attack and one of you would have to come and bring back my body."

Should it become necessary, Junior would probably be the one stuck with that task. The girls would patch up their differences, band together and force him to go.

Cecile said, "That <u>would</u> be the worst!"

"Because of the inconvenience?"

"Mother!" Helen now. "You think we don't care about what happens to you?"

Maryanne was glad to have drawn their fire. Maybe the way to reunify the family was for her to run away, willful and mad with devilment as the three-year-olds you see with their hands up over their heads powering their little legs pell-mell down the aisles of the supermarket.

Helen confronted her later in the kitchen. "Mother?" She paused. "Can you tell me what this is all about?"

Maryanne's turn to pause. Then, as simply as she could make it sound while still hiding how hurt she felt, she said, "I have the rest of my life to make up and none of my children seem to approve of my first stabs at doing that."

Did they find her frivolous? Or was she really somehow out of line, demanding too much of them? In the family mythology, the demanding one had been Giles. Her role had been to deal with the children's father's moody complaining so they could stay free to have their childhoods. Maryanne the one who had packed up household after household while Giles hopscotched from university to university looking for a department where they would stroke him and put up with all his quirks at the same time. The footlooseness of the father eventually became a family joke, an acceptable way of referring to Giles Fort's massive insecurity. Helen was as smart as any of the brood and attached to her dad, but she was also Maryanne's ally. They often took heart together, smoothing Giles's feathers in relay and all the while laughing at him a little behind his back.

Junior and his crew returned from skiing the first of January. Two weeks later on a bitterly cold, blue-sky Sunday they came up to collect their presents and consume a big chicken Maryanne had fixed. When the meal was over, she drew Junior into the den and told him she needed to make out a new will.

"Why, Mother? There's not something wrong, is there?"

"No, but I went and got the old one out of the lock box and discovered currently I'm leaving everything to Giles."

"Yes, but there <u>are</u> provisions for after Dad's decease, aren't there?"

Her son was so much taller than she—he loomed over her--that Maryanne sometimes had trouble contradicting him.

"Of course. But it's so out of date some of the grandkids, including your children, aren't even mentioned or left anything."

Well then of course, Junior agreed, it was time. He had a young associate who could do the drafting.

"Not you?"

"I was presuming. Sorry. Am I not _in_ your will, Mom?"

She laughed. "Oh of course you are, silly."

What Maryanne didn't say was that she was thinking now of an unequal split. The house to all four of them, of course. Maybe the practical problem of figuring out how to get the price they deserved for a three-bedroom Victorian with a cupola and porches and an ample Midwestern backyard would bring the children back together. But beyond that she was thinking mainly of keepsakes and furniture for Junior and the two older girls. The ready cash should go to Rennie, the only one who still needed financial propping up, and then the rest of the estate in trust for the grandkids' education.

"Mom?" Junior was all smiles. "You wouldn't consider putting off this new Chiapas trip until Rennie's ready to go with you, would you?"

"Rennie's plan is Oaxaca, not Chiapas."

"Yes, but--"

"And going with Rennie would mean Eric, of course. Does Rennie actually have a plan yet?"

"No."

Maryanne let his word hang there. A shrug, a look. Junior didn't press.

"A funny thing happened. That day I went to Manantiales, in the night really, just as we were about to leave the village...."

Junior's face settled into a professional look--a very expensive one, she was aware--so she couldn't say he wasn't paying attention. But it was also clear he wasn't disposed to listen to any charming tales from the drug- or rebel-infested hinterlands of southern Mexico.

She went on anyway. "Just as we were about to leave the village they came running to us. I had to get out of the car. Someone had a list, a *cuenta*. They showed it to me by flashlight. It was an inventory, really, things Dad and I had packed up the first time we left. Forty years ago! Pots and pans, a little Coleman stove, rat traps, things like that. Well yes, I told them, that <u>was</u> our list. I recognized my own handwriting, much more legible then than it is now. But what about it? Well, they wanted to know, what did I want done with the things? They still had them and they wanted to take me to see them. But there wasn't time, the people I had come with were anxious to get back to San Cristóbal. So I told the neighbors I would divide up the goods when I came back. So you see, I more or less committed myself to--"

"Forty-two."

"Forty-two what?"

"It's now closer to forty-two years ago that you and Dad went there."

"Oh yes, of course." They were back in the kitchen. Down the hall Maryanne could see Junior's wife and his boys getting on their bright parkas, rows of chairlift tickets dangling from the drawstrings like Eskimo amulets. Eat up and hurry back down to the city as quick as possible. It seemed to be the only way they had of dealing with her.

"So when I got back to the hotel I dreamed I was at the hospital again and they brought Dad's final bill. Remember that incredible thing? One hundred-and-two thousand dollars for nine days was it? Except in the dream it was the inventory of pots and pans, in my handwriting."

"The reckoning."

"Yes." Maryanne had not thought of that. The practice of law had done no harm to Junior's old talent for analogies and metaphors. Had there been a poet in the family it would have been him. Maryanne went on, "And the doctors who presented it to me were all in their scrubs and huge, like those overwhelming giant puppets at Carnavál in Veracruz? Remember the time we went to see that?"

"No Mom, I don't." Junior pushed past her into the hall to get his own jacket. He stopped and looked down. "Yeah," he admitted, "I do remember those puppets. They scared me. What is it you think? That after forty-some years for some reason you still owe these people something?"

"No." Although she was pleased with the interpretation, and to herself she said, *Maybe I do, yes.*

Maryanne's ticket for Mexico City was for Groundhog's Day. The afternoon after Helen and her husband departed on their opera-lovers' tour, Maryanne made a trip up to their house. Their sons were staying with the families of their high school friends and a neighbor was responsible for the cat and tapping the dried-shrimp morsels into the goldfish bowl every five days.

But Maryanne had a key to let herself in. When she noticed she was tiptoeing, she laughed at herself. The heat had been left at 55, wasteful in Maryanne's view but the temperature at which Helen had determined her houseplants would stay comfy.

Maryanne went into the back pantry and opened two lower cupboard doors at the far end. She set the cardboard box with the metal-reenforced corners on top of a dozen Kerr canning jars bound tight with plastic wrap. Their nomadic years trekking from university to university had made Helen as a grownup a person for whom schedules were holy writ. If Maryanne wasn't back by mid-June, Helen would find the major portion of her father's ashes when apricots from the west became available in North Shore supermarkets.

Once her flight the next morning was under way, she started thinking about Rosie Tu'ul and the confidence she shared with Maryanne on her last trip. Rosie's daughter Alejandra, who was 12 or about to be 12, wanted to dress more like her school friends and begin to wear a little lipstick and eye-liner. Rosie thought it was too soon for make-up, and Sr. Utrillo made the mistake of saying in their miniskirts and their tube tops the girl's friends looked like little *putas*. Alejandra told her mother that under the surface she was still really just a stupid <u>Indian</u> and Rosie slapped her and then felt ashamed of herself. When they caught Alejandra all packed up and about to run away, she was put on house detention. Sr. Utrillo took it upon himself to accompany his daughter to school every morning and to wait for her outside the building when classes let out in the afternoon. When Rosie asked Maryanne what to do, Maryanne shook her head and said she was sorry, she herself had still not become wise about her own children even though they were all grown by now. Really? Rosie seemed heartened by her older friend's admission. Her own mother couldn't help, she said, because the kind of waywardness Alejandra was showing (her *rebeldía* Rosie called it*)* wasn't something that occurred in "the village" yet, at least not among the girls. When Maryanne told Rosie a slightly milder version of the charges Rennie was given to leveling against her, Rosie seemed shocked. But Maryanne quickly added that her youngest was actually a fine person and that Rosie might meet her some day soon since Rennie was now again considering SanCris as a place to work on her Spanish.

Texas went by and they were across the border. Not a cloud in the sky and 38,000 feet below the almost white deserts of Chihuahua, punctuated with tiny spots of green where the farming towns were. Maryanne dozed. Then woke suddenly. The new will, her putting in for her own retirement from the university in June, leaving the box at Helen's-- What if the children put two and two together and read her wrong? She admitted to a desire to disappear for a while, but not to any suicidal impulse. She had recently decided what she was going to do with the ashes might be the real focus of the kids' anxiety--or at least of Helen's. What harm could their dotty old mom do, unless it was to leave difficult dad's mortal remains in a place far from them and among people they despised?

CB

San Cristóbal's official altitude is seventy-five hundred feet, Manantiales is mostly above eight thousand. There in the thinner atmosphere the raggedy puffs of cloud that race across the sky often produce shadows like living hands chasing things unseen across the green meadows and fields.

Sitting at the top of the valley with the other women watching sheep one day, Maryanne found herself pushing to revise the story of what had happened to her career. It remained true that she had been wrong to trust Giles and the world and to imagine her role in their work would be recognized even without her name on a book cover. But it was also true that her ambition was different from her husband's, not less exactly, but certainly less pointed. As time went by, Giles came to seem more and more goaded along by demons while Maryanne felt she always had time to look down byways. Though getting pregnant the first time and each of the following times were the major factors, the very view before her now had had a part in her decision to go a little slower than her importunate young husband. She had a friend, a prominent Mexican novelist, who said it was ironic but carrying a child made her feel moribund and nearly crazy. Though Maryanne sympathized, producing babies never sapped her energy, at least not until the harder time she had at 38 with Rennie. Pregnancy did make her complacent, though, gave her a feeling that for the moment just her being was enough, was all that really mattered.

She was staying with Losha and Marta. Rosie's brother had come and constructed a second wooden bed in the corner opposite the one where Losha and her granddaughter slept. The arrangement suited Maryanne. Giles's stricture about having your own place where you could shut the door no longer seemed relevant. Maryanne did, however, make a point of not becoming cut off from the rest of Manantiales. Every day she walked down into "town" to buy something or do some wash at the river, or just to stop in and visit at households where she knew people. She wasn't sure, but there was a chance that maintaining her own social ties down the hill would help keep in check the jealousy and suspicions which seemed to cling to Losha. Maryanne herself had no doubts. If Losha <u>was</u> a witch, her magic and her intentions were certainly directed entirely toward doing others good.

Though Maryanne had been in Manantiales for less than a month, sometimes it felt as though she had been back forever. She was adapted to the diet again, hardly missed meat, kept most intestinal bugs at bay. She had found a way to give herself an adequate bath with buckets of hot water in the clearing behind Losha's house. And as Losha had promised, with fair regularity the two of them heated rocks in the fire and went in the tiny lean-to against the house to sweat and gossip and switch themselves with good-smelling branches. From time to time Marta would come in, shy about their half-covered old bodies, and sling a bucket of water on the hot stones for them.

Maryanne was amused by the way the community willed her to act like a grandmother. There was symmetry here. When she was 24 the women would comment to one another that it was well past time for Maryanne to become a mother. Now as she neared 70, they talked about her "acting her age" (in Maya the phrase was fond, not censorious). Little children of both sexes were pushed off onto her, kids not yet fully weaned. The grownups expected her to know how to amuse them, babysit them, quickly lift them up and hold them outside the door of the house when they looked like they were about to spout pee.

She seemed to fit in as a grandmother better here than she did in Wilmette. The time she got with her own grandkids was programmed almost to the minute because they had schedules that had to fit like neat smaller boxes inside the boxes of their parents' hectic schedules. Even when they were enjoying one another's company, Maryanne was aware of how quickly her grandsons might become bored and ask could they go watch TV or take out their video games now. Here, the kids soon found out there were likely to be paper and Crayons in Maryanne's net bag, and they drew and proudly presented her the results with no prompting. An almost embarrassingly easy way to collect data. After only three weeks, she had pieces by grandchildren and even great-grandchildren of many of the people in her original study. Not much concerted comparison she could do without the old pictures before her, but she could sense already there would be things worth saying about the differences in the images. Television and the years two-thirds of the Mexican army had spent in the highlands had left their mark. Boys drew more cars and tanks, more planes shooting bullets and superheroes in capes, the girls women in short ladina-style skirts with bright red lips.

In the beginning, of course, everyone asked 'How long are you going to stay?' It was a question Manantiales etiquette demanded. But now that she had settled in, Maryanne met fewer and fewer people she hadn't just seen the day before or the day before that. And once you became a regular, the question was not asked again. She paid Losha for her food and a little extra for her lodging, and contributed to the household things she found to buy--bananas, oranges--or food gifts other people pressed on her—bean tamales, bags of homegrown peanuts, large handfuls of gathered greens. There was no question Losha was glad to have her. In fact, early one morning just when they were about to go higher up into the mountains to cut firewood, she made a little speech thanking Maryanne for coming and alleviating what Losha called in Tzeltal her 'widow's burden of being alone.'

Just as it had in the old days, news ran around the community at a speed that perplexed Maryanne. She and Giles had never been able to figure out the networks, so for them Manantiales gossip came to have an almost supernatural aspect. Not only did other people know your every movement, often they appeared to know what you were about to do before you did. ("So you are going to be at the house blessing ceremony tomorrow." "Am I? I didn't know.") The single telephone at the schoolhouse extended the range of the gossip system as far as San Cristóbal, but some people now even had cell phones and could speak at any moment to their sons looking for work in Tennessee or Georgia. Though Losha hardly ever went down the hill herself, she seemed to know precisely when Rosa and her husband were coming out from town to see her. Maryanne remained mystified about this until she realized when the granddaughter Marta went down to visit her parents, which she did nearly every day, she brought back messages for Losha from her kin.

But still, it seemed that in her years Losha was motivated much less by information than she was by intuition. She was often in a kind of prayer state while also present and in useful touch with reality. The old lady's split consciousness reminded Maryanne of people who could talk with you and follow the TV program across the room at the same time.

Currently, she seemed concerned with getting away from the house. Last night she had proposed the three of them go into the mountains at first light to collect firewood, although the present supply of split pieces lined up under the eaves was more than adequate. But when they woke up at four a.m. in the dead dark it was raining heavily and Losha said they could go back to sleep. The rain cleared off by mid-morning and the sun came out but by then the firewood expedition was apparently on hold. At noon Losha had Marta hardboiling eggs while she herself made tortillas for what sounded like an overnight expedition to visit some crosses and what Losha called vaguely "a cave where we go to pray sometimes."

Maryanne was perfectly willing to go along, though it was unclear whether they would be sleeping out--maybe in the shelter of the cave's mouth?--or staying the night in someone's house. There was a reason for Losha to be so avid to get away for a while. There was a "job" (a <u>cargo</u> or burden they called it in Spanish) which was supposed to go to a woman of some years, preferably one who had not married. But since marriage was more or less universal in Manantiales, the cargo was quite often bestowed on a widow. The woman who took it on became responsible for counting and repairing the clothing and all the jingly necklaces of old coins, the silver crown of the Virgin, mirrors, scepters, ribbons, and other paraphernalia that were the possessions of the wood and plaster saints housed in the Ermita. There were boxes and boxes of these effects, kept in different officials' houses, the clothes changed throughout the year for the different fiestas. Maryanne was unsure how much actual work was involved, but the "Widow's Work" as it was sometimes called was very important to the community, and always spoken of as being hugely onerous. Maryanne had heard other women talking up Losha as the right person for the job. They praised her weaving and her embroidery, which had always been considered of the highest quality, and seemed mostly concerned about how long the old lady's strength might remain with her. No mention of any purported truck with dark magic, at least not in the gringa's presence.

If Losha was the one they chose, there would be a ceremony, a *pedida* modeled on the way you asked for a girl's hand in marriage. A large number of people would come and surround Losha's little house in the night. Two a.m. was the preferred hour. There would be musicians with violins and drums and men with their heads wrapped in gray bandanas dancing with rattles, and male and female "petitioners" on their knees at the front door. They would remain there several hours begging in whiny, singsong voices for Losha to come outside and agree to become the "Holy Mother/Wife to the Little Saints." In the end, if she did accept, Losha would appear at the door acting surprised and gratified and proclaim her unworthiness. The petitioners would brush her objections aside in elegant long phrases and invade the house and <u>demand</u> she accept--which she then would. (In the marriage version, it was the girl's parents who facetiously deprecated their daughter's skills at weaving and cooking.)

But the pedida was a one-shot thing. If Losha wasn't home the night they came, then the petitioners were supposed to truck off to some other woman's house and begin the whole procedure over. The idea was that once the "courting" process began, it had to go on until the town had secured a new Holy Mother/ Wife.

Starting after 1:30 in the afternoon, the two old ladies and the girl traveled slowly up into the mountains, Maryanne going first on the path and Losha clinging to the back of her blouse, Marta bringing up the rear. The weather held, cool, the air damp, the sky blue and cotton-swab clouds going by, no more rain in sight. The crosses and the cave Losha wanted to visit were not that much higher up, so there was not really much climbing to do. The paths were muddy and slick, however, and demanded taking care. When she spotted even a mildly iffy place to put your foot, Marta called forward to Maryanne and her grandmother, "<u>K'unk'un ta k'unk'un</u>," meaning 'Slowly, slowly.'

Which after a while caused Maryanne to notice that the dropping away sensation, the entrance into emptiness she had experienced after Giles's death, had also dropped away from her unnoticed. When did that happen? Had there been any of it since the afternoon Losha burned Giles's two ID cards? It seemed not.

Around a bend suddenly they came on the cave opening. The mouth was symmetrically arched, fifteen or twenty feet high, spindly trees clinging to the rocks above it. Maryanne and Losha sat on a log by the entrance and shared a gourd bowl of water while Marta took a flashlight and sticks of reddish pine heartwood *ocote* out of her pack. The cave gave off breath, a cold smell like molding leaves, and there was an echoing distant gurgle Maryanne assumed must be a stream or underground river deep inside. Marta went ahead with the flashlight and the two older women came along behind holding up burning lengths of pine that sizzled and popped and dripped hot resin. Maryanne was surprised. The cave interior was not that high-ceilinged, but it had some stalactites and stalagmites, and many divisions and byways, and long patches of limestone wall made marbly smooth and white by the seepage of water. The floor was fairly regular and smooth, but little streams crossed it in places, and there were some big puddles to edge around. Despite her blindness, as they moved deeper in the old woman seemed to know exactly where she was going.

They came to crosses, some freshly painted blue, older, more beat-up ones behind tilted against the side of the cavern. There was a low wooden table in front of the crosses which clearly was there to serve as an altar. The ground here was dry, so once Losha had bent and placed an even row of her candles and lit them, they doubled their rebozos and got down on their knees and the old woman began to pray.

Her own feeling about caves Maryanne liked to think was fairly Mayan in its way. She was a little scared by them yet drawn to them at the same time. For the Maya caves were the access to the underworld, to a territory which in the sacred text called the Popol Vuh was named Xibalbá. It was a place that aroused all the same dread and fascination bad dreams do.

The scholars said the Popol Vuh was probably written out from pictorial guides used by storytellers among what they called the Quiché Elite in Guatemala soon after the arrival of the Spanish. Gnomic, almost impenetrable in its Spanish version, in the beginning it had little attraction for the young Forts in their fieldwork. Only after Maryanne's friend Munro Edmundson published his beautiful English version called The Book of Counsel did Maryanne and Giles see how closely certain Popul Vuh episodes mirrored tales they told in Manantiales. And the book's point of view on the way of the world was also very like their villagers'. It is a tricky place, full of pitfalls, our life. You have to be alert and inventive to get through it, but honesty and decency also count.

In the underworld the Popol Vuh describes there is the heart-thumping possibility at any moment of meeting up with the terrifying, loutish Lords of Xibalbá, an all-male contingent with a charming preoccupation with dead things, with spreading disease, and a lurid reveling in putrescence. Once you got across a river of writhing scorpions you might suddenly face a slimy river of slow-flowing blood. (Yuck-o! as the Fort children would say.) Or you might get locked in the House of Freelance Razors with the deadly blades zooming at you out of nowhere all night long. Land there and you could kiss any hope of peaceful dreams goodbye.

But actually, the tests a human being must pass in the Mayan netherworld of the <u>Popol Vuh</u> are ludicrously simple ones. Just act like those very clever boys, the so-called Hero Twins, and keep your thinking cap on. The fearsome Lords of Xibalbá? The Scabber? Mr. Pus? Pushovers, easily thwarted, quickly duped. In the end, bozos, comic-book villains. Tales of the underworld may make a little child's hair stand on end, but to a woman who has survived five decades of academia and come out Distinguished Professor the macabre funhouse of Xibalbá would be a piece of cake.

ങ

They slept by the fire at the home of some people nearby (the wife seemed to be a niece of some sort) and got back to Losha's the next day around noon. After they had built up the fire a little and eaten something, the old lady sent her granddaughter outside, 'To have a look around,' as she put it. Marta returned to report she had seen no signs of anyone having come by the house while they were gone. Maryanne felt confirmed in her suspicion that Losha had been so intent on going on the pilgrimage to avoid the petitioners coming about the Widow's Work.

But then in the dead of night she woke to a rustling sound. At first she thought the rain had returned, the noise just a little shower passing through their clearing. Then silence. Or maybe it was an animal outside, a raccoon or a weasal or a possum. Silence again. Her new wristwatch had a luminous face and it was nearby, but when she found it the greenish hands glowed too weakly for her to be sure of the time. Maryanne lay back, eyes open, trying to see the soot-draped pole rafters overhead. A memory appeared, half a dream. It was the day she and Giles hoisted their old notes up to store overhead in the garage at the Wilmette house. Giles was up above on the plywood platform saying, 'Do you want these?' and pointing to some rolls of age-browned newsprint. 'Yes, leave them,' said Maryanne. 'Whatever are you going to do with them?' he insisted, falling back into that midwestern flatness he had once worked so hard to get out of his speech. Maryanne was insistent back. 'I don't know. All I know is that I do want them! So hands off, Giles, please!'

Full awake again, staring up into the darkness. In real life, what had happened? There had been a quarrel. Giles called her a packrat. Maryanne said, not very originally, that he should talk. Then, calming down, she suggested they should each choose something they thought valuable and throw it away and that way they'd double the space available.

And in the end? She remembered turning to go back in the house, how loud the gravel crunched under her heel. But after that--?

She couldn't remember. She didn't stay angry, did she? Didn't come out an hour later and get the ladder and bring down her hundreds of children's drawings and burn them or take them and stuff them in the trash bin herself. Or did she? She remembered many little piles of smoldering, smoky leaves, herself leaning on a rake watching the flames lick up, die back, burn up brighter again. An acrid smell but not the smell of newsprint.

Now distinctly there were voices outside, whispers and more rustling, the silvery strings of a harp being tuned, the impatient thump of a thumb against a drum head. The girl Marta was up cupping a flashlight in her hand, moving about, the red glow darting and flitting like the cigar ends the Hero Twins fashion out of fireflies to fool the Lords in one of their tests. Losha herself was hurriedly getting into her blue skirt when the banging on the door and the shouts and whining of the excited crowd outside began.

It was two hours almost before Losha cracked the door and allowed the petitioners to push in and surround her. The sun was coming up--another two hours--before Losha, fairly drunk by then, began to make the speeches where she agreed to take on the work in honor of the little saints. Appropriate tears were streaming from the ancient lady's smoky eyes. But she was grinning too.

Maryanne was also quite drunk by then, sitting on a little stool in an honor position at the head of the women's contingent. Though the music and some of the official thanksgivings continued, lighter talk and laughter had begun too. And strangers had rekindled the cooking fire and a meal they had brought was about to be served.

The neighbor seated next to her leaned toward Maryanne. "Did you know your daughter came looking for you yesterday?"

Maryanne first thought she meant 'daughter' metaphorically. "Ah yes, my Rosie," she said.

"No, your own real daughter, the blond one." The neighbor laughed and swayed a little closer. "With the <u>big</u> husband."

Maryanne put her head back and laughed. "And the <u>big</u> hands too?" she said. "That one?"

All the women around them were laughing now and making little murmuring comments. "If it was <u>that</u> big--" one of them said, eyes widening.

Poor Eric. So earnest in his floundering way. How uncomfortable he would be if he knew that, whatever its real dimensions, a gaggle of Mayan women had been joking about his penis.

Strange. Had the older children finally chosen Rennie to come looking for their wayward mother? Maryanne believed Rennie and Eric were capable of getting themselves to Chiapas on their own. But all the way out to Manantiales? Maybe they managed to find Rosie Tu'ul and she had helped them.

"What did you tell them?" Maryanne asked the woman next to her.

"We said we hadn't seen you."

Drunk self found that very funny, could see Rennie's look first of confusion, then her hardening eyes, her conviction that these people were lying--just the kind of treatment she should have figured she'd get in this wretched place.

"Did she say she would come again?"

"I don't know. I wasn't the one who talked with her."

For once, observer self was nodding and agreeing with drunk self. She had not only been taken in by Manantiales, now they had seen fit to hide her from her own. Back, return. *How many times,* she was singing to herself, *how many times will I have to return?*

She hadn't remembered she knew the next verse of the song, which answered the question. Her woozy head sang on, *If it could be forever, that's how long I would return for.*

☙

The hotel Rennie and Eric had gone to on Janice Metz's advice was right in the center of town, one of the several dozen which had expectantly opened their doors since Maryanne's day. These hostels served the endless straggle of European and now Asian young who trucked through San Cristóbal on their way to ruins or jungles or water rafting, to perdition or just to Guatemala. In the dark entryway, the managers, a diminutive older couple, seemed confused on several levels. Had Maryanne not come looking for a room? Was a hundred and fifty pesos too much? It had its own shower, plenty of hot water. There were rooms with shared bathrooms at one twenty-five if she preferred. And the young people, Maryanne asked, the woman with the big hair (she demonstrated by making a large imaginary ball around her own head) and the man with the dark beard and (well, she might as well say it), the big stomach? Oh, them! Well. The little couple exchanged glances. <u>Maybe</u>, yes, they were probably in their room. Maryanne was free to go up and look for them if she wanted. It was one of the last two rooms, up on the third floor, number 15. The couple had asked for it especially.

The stairwell was brightened by a large skylight overhead. Climbing to the second floor and going along past open doors which gave little vignettes of nicely-made beds and clean towels laid out, Maryanne's opinion of the place improved. Someone here liked bleach and soap and meticulously swept floors. And if you liked everything around you painted either blue or a psychedelic tangerine painful to the eye, this might indeed be your place.

In the back, lit by a second, smaller skylight, an even steeper set of stairs to the third floor. Maryanne was paused for breath with her hand on the banister when a metal door above clicked open with a hollow sound and a man's deep voice said, "Well OK, see you around then," and a moment later Eric came into view, larger-seeming than ever in a big yellow down jacket and trailing a suitcase on wheels from which dangled a number of black straps. The plastic fasteners at their ends scraped and chattered along the tiles. Not noticing Maryanne, Eric turned and started backing the suitcase down the stairs, clunk, clunk, clunk. At the landing where he stopped to let out a big breath he finally saw her.

"What the fuck?"

Maryanne took her time. Always take your time with people when they're upset. "Hello, Eric. Nice to see you."

"Yeah, sure," he said, and went back to backing down the stairs bumping his luggage after him. When he got to Maryanne, he was sweating and puffing and red-faced. She could smell him, not an unpleasant smell, some aftershave maybe, soap?

"Where the hell were you?"

"I— What do you mean?"

"We came looking for you and you weren't there. In the village. Rennie freaked."

"And you?"

"Me?" He thought about it dolefully, sighed. "Me, I am just beyond caring anymore."

"Oh, OK," she said. "Going out?"

"You bet I am. To Guatemala. Where I should have gone in the first place. See you around. Or not."

And he turned and went trundling along toward the farther stairs. Maryanne watched for a little, the big rounded shoulders hunched up toward where his ears would be if they weren't mostly hidden in his curly locks, the mincing dance-like way a big man sometimes walks, on the balls of his feet. Even after he had disappeared down the stairs, his smell lingered in the back hall. Eric must have showered before his departure, using that rose-scented soap that comes in little pink individual bars in lower-end Mexican hotels.

"The Last of Eric"? It could be the title of a picture.

Then from above distantly what sounded like a kitten mewing.

Maryanne went on up, slowly, clutching the banister. At the top, two windows and two metal doors along the walkway. She peered first to the right: a covered laundry area, tubs, a hand-crank wringer, plants in tin cans and, beyond, a kind of cement terrace, sunlight, tile roofs, trees.

One of the metal doors stood very slightly ajar. Maryanne rapped lightly and pushed in. Rennie sat at the head of the bed with a big wad of pink toilet paper up to her nose, wearing just a very big, somewhat dirty-looking t-shirt which said NOISE! in large black letters. The bed looked as though it had been the ring for a wrestling match, the covers jumbled off onto the floor, one of the pillows down too, the bottom sheet pulled back exposing the mattress.

Here another pervasive smell. Oil, garlic. Had they been having take-out pizza at some point? Or grinders maybe?

Rennie watched her mother over the big wad of paper but didn't say anything. Her teary eyes showed no surprise, no affection, but no anger or reproach either.

"I seem to have arrived at the wrong moment," Maryanne said.

This provoked from Rennie a big tremble and then a kind of low howl and a fresh flow of tears. When she took the toilet paper away to look for a dry area so she could blot, her mouth alarmed her mother. It was red and smeary, as though Rennie had been stuffing herself with raspberries.

"What's going on with your mouth, honey? You're not bleeding, are you?"

Rennie pulled the toilet paper away again and stared at it. There was red there too.

"No," she laughed a little. "Lipstick. We went out to eat and to a bar last night to hear music and I got all done up to go."

It sounded so unlike Rennie, who hardly used make-up. But now Maryanne could see her eyes had had some blue liner on them recently, and maybe a little pencil in her eyebrows as well.

Before Maryanne could ask, Rennie shrugged and said, "I don't know why...."

Up a little step in the back of the room was a bathroom in the same blue tile and bright orange combination as the rest of the hotel. "Honey," Maryanne said, "before anything else, I have to pee. Is it all right?"

"Be my guest," and Rennie made a kind of ladylike but dismissive gesture in the direction of the bathroom.

Door closed, Maryanne sat on the somewhat small toilet, pushing down a little on herself so she could be sure the urine was hitting the water in the bowl. Her pubic hair was once very thick, the whole area much admired by the great Giles Fort (though true enough in the era before greatness was thrust upon him). Now gray, the patch still thick enough, crinkly. Her bush.

A word she knew many women minded, but she never had.

Why such thoughts?

Because of sex. Rennie's room smelled heavily of it. Maryanne laughed at herself. Had it been so long that she couldn't recognize it and would think Italian food instead?

CB

Rennie remained upset, but since Maryanne <u>was</u> her mother and willing to sit on the corner of the bed and listen, at least for the moment her being gone when they came looking for her in the village had to take a back seat to other grievances. It seemed Maryanne was only the latest in a list of people who had disappointed Rennie and Eric, 'fucked with us' as she put it. They had skipped seeing Mexico City in order to get to San Cristóbal on the overnight bus so they could meet up with friends from Chicago by a certain date. But then days and days passed and the friends didn't show, never even emailed. Nothing. No consideration. And Rennie and Eric had no one to contact except that old lady. ("Janice, you mean," Maryanne put in. "Yeah, her," said Rennie.) Finally yesterday they went out early and signed up for a month's worth of Spanish lessons at a place Janice had recommended and then took the bus out to Manantiales. ('Your old place,' she called it.) And when they got back empty-handed, there were their friends waiting for them all sunburned and peeling and expecting her and Eric to be glad to see them. It seemed they'd found this waterfall down the road at a place called Agua Azul or something where the swimming was good and the living easy so they had just decided to stay there a while.

(Knowing Agua Azul herself, Maryanne could imagine how the thundering cascades might well beguile the weary travelers and delay them on their journey. She didn't mention this to Rennie, however.)

After the friends, Rennie said, she and Eric agreed they needed to try to recoup, get the spirit of adventure back. While she was getting dressed, he went out and came back with a little bouquet of white flowers for her, then they got into their best duds and went to eat and to look for some music. All good. But what Eric saved for this morning was the news that while he was on the search for the flowers he also dropped by the language school and got his deposit back. He didn't want Rennie to think badly of him, he said, but he was going to have to bail.

By this point in her recitation, Rennie's face had clouded over again. Sniffles turned suddenly to renewed full-scale weeping.

Maryanne reached over and held Rennie's bare foot for a long moment until the crying slowed.

"And you know what he asked then?"

"No, honey, what?"

"He wanted to make love. As a kind of I don't know what—a gesture I guess."

"And?"

Rennie shrugged. "What the hell? I said OK. So we did. And in fact it was all right. When we were done he got up, packed his stuff, showered and left. And that was the moment you decided to put in an appearance."

The girl found her toilet paper and blew her nose into it. She hauled herself up off the bed, straightened her t-shirt, and indicating the bathroom said, "I got to go in there myself."

Maryanne waited, glad to have a little time alone. The toilet flushed, then came the sound of the shower. She herself had gone directly from the Mantaniales combi to Janice's and then had come on here. So when Rennie pushed open the door and stepped down out of the bathroom, her body a bright rosy color in the midst of a cloud of steam, Maryanne asked did she think there might be any hot water left.

"There's plenty, Mom. It's the best thing about this place."

"Do you think I could clean up a little myself then?"

"Be my guest. We brought an extra towel." She turned and bent over her suitcase. "In here somewhere, unless <u>he</u> took it."

But Eric had left the towel behind, and after Maryanne had bathed, trying Rennie's shampoo and using up the slippery nubbin of the little pink soap provided, mother and daughter went through Rennie's things in search of something Maryanne might be able to wear to lunch at Janice's. What they came up with was first a somewhat faded wrap-around denim skirt mother had given daughter so long ago she had forgotten it, then a skimpy silk t-shirt and a man's pin-striped suit vest Rennie had gotten at Goodwill.

Maryanne went out onto the azotea drying her hair with the towel. The view from there was open and grand. Straight ahead the patchwork of dirty reddish roofs of the lower half of San Cristóbal and beyond them the hazy mass of Huitepec, the mountain which looms over the western portion of the city. To Maryanne's right emerging from palms and shade trees large yellow slices of the side-by-side domes of La Caridad and Santo Domingo, two of the town's oldest churches. And back of them

Cerrillo, the barrio named after its hill, a steep-rising ridge. Up there toward the top somewhere, hard to pick out for sure, Janice and Lois's house.

Joining Maryanne in the sun, Rennie took her mother's damp towel and offered her a big green plastic comb. A little wind had sprung up. The sheets on the line behind them swayed and rustled.

"Quiet up here."

"I know. Very quiet for being right in the middle of town. In the morning, early, there're church bells, and sometimes at night those sky rockets go off—"

"*Cohetes.*"

"Right. And maybe some dogs barking. But otherwise—"

"And," said Maryanne, "you have turtles."

"We do? Where?"

Maryanne led Rennie back into the shaded area where the washing was done and pointed out the low tin tub in the corner with the two small flat green turtles in it. Sensing something above them, the little creatures feathered their front fins and moved a bit, then were still again.

CB

How did Janice know to recommend those third-floor rooms in the little hotel? They couldn't have been a recent discovery of hers because since the time of her hip and the big cast she wouldn't have been able to manage all those stairs.

But how like her to have such facts. Lois had been the same. People who didn't get on with them gave the ladies a reputation for being nosy, but Maryanne and Giles saw it differently. Janet and Lois always shook their heads over 'anthropology.' What was it anyway? they would demand in their best confrontive, chin-forward style. And no matter what you came up with, they would probably sniff at you or laugh or shake their heads. But Giles, clever man, one time seemed to get to them. "Social anthropology," he said, "is a somewhat inept attempt to make something regular out of our natural human curiosity. You know, the kind of poking around you two are so devoted to."

There were things about San Cristóbal the ladies had learned which local people would confirm should you ask but no other gringo might ever have figured out. Surprising facts to interfere with your beliefs about the hard-heartedness of the place's ladinos. Maryanne's favorite was the one about the brick factory. Though no longer in operation, the brick-firing plant still stood out at what had once been the edge of town, its wooden sheds, always ramshackle, now falling to pieces. But the heart of the operation remained, a huge wood-burning kiln lined with rock and covered with such a quantity of earth it looked almost like a natural hillock sprung up in the middle of the field. Grass grew on it almost to the top. And back in the day when they were still making bricks, Janice reported, on cold nights the owners would let people with no place else to go—

beggars and the lowest-end prostitutes—come in and sleep on
the still-warm mound of the kiln.

☙

Comida, the mid-day meal, had always been Janice and
Lois's big ticket. "Come by one-thirty and we'll eat by two," they
would say. You might also be invited to drop over for the evening,
but that was always a lesser occasion. Guests for comida were
chosen in clusters that might be expected to produce not only
talk but maybe also some clash of opinions. Only Janice had
been a card-carrying Party member, but Lois also appreciated
dialectic, enlightenment through controversy, the arrival at a
soothing synthesis by the end of the afternoon as a possibility
but not required. The tall, elegant Algerian agronomist Paul
Coeytaux once spread his long arms and complimented Janice
and Lois for having managed to produce a salon right here in
San Cristóbal. "Oh no," both ladies cried, "us?" though you
could tell from their poor attempts at hiding their smiles how
happy Paul made them.

Though he was fairly sure he had toted it up right, Rufus
Bright still wondered could it really be 35 years he had been
coming here. What he remembered—and sometimes retold
Janice—was a borscht Lois served the first time he was invited,
a soup so rich, giving off its earthy smells even as the plates were
being ghosted to the table carefully so as not to slosh them, that
his stomach growled. In those days, except at Trudi Blom's table
at Na Bolom and a couple of hole-in-the-walls in the old market,

a visitor could find almost no good food in San Cristóbal. All through the meal, Lois kept apologizing for having been unable to find sour cream for the borscht and the guests kept demurring saying <u>oh no no, it's fine, Lois!</u> while busily shoveling it down. Sour cream would have been nice, but certainly wasn't necessary. By the end of the meal Rufus found himself entered into a kind of daze in which from moment to moment he forgot he was deep in the bowels of Mexico.

Today he and Janice spent the morning on the big cardboard box which contained all her negatives and contact sheets. Cataloguing her materials was an ongoing project, Rufus pulling items and Janice scrutinizing what he handed over to her, assigning dates and years, names of people when she could remember them, anecdotes about the trouble she had with this shot or that, the various serendipities. ("I was just going for the sunlight spilling in on the interior of that little church in Mitontic—gone, now, you know, they tore it down--and at the last moment those three small boys snuck in the front door to find out what in heck I was up to and them standing there, well, they made the picture.")

He kept notes.

And luckily from the very beginning so had she. Coming late to photography from a career as an architectural draftsman, Janice had been meticulous. All the contact sheets were enveloped together with the right negatives, and there was also a clear coding system to link them. She had written down exposure times as well, and annotations on how the shots she chose to enlarge should be printed.

Through Rufus's good offices the Newberry Library in Chicago had agreed to take the entire collection. No money was offered, but the selling point was obvious: an outfit like the Newberry would preserve her negatives in excellent condition for the foreseeable future. Since Janice wasn't making prints any more, Rufus assumed once they were through with this task she would allow him to hand carry the box back to the States. Or maybe she would want to hang onto it and the transfer would have to wait until after she went off to rejoin Lois. Janice's attitude toward the box changed regularly. Some days when Rufus brought it out from under the bed in her room, she would wave at it dismissively and say, "Who cares anyway? It's not as though I ever sold a lot, you know. Or was published much either. In the long run who's going to want to look at this stuff?" Other days when he was sent to get the box, Rufus would find that she had secreted it away in some different place. He discovered it once under the sink in her darkroom, another time in the bottom of the pine armoire where she hung her clothes. And sometimes when visitors came to the house unexpectedly, she would tell him, "Quick! Put everything away! That box over there in the corner and that cloth over it!"

Rufus would tell people he lacked the toilet training ever to become much of an archivist. But now, especially since Javier's departure, he found himself agreeing to do more of it. Somehow his partner's death had put a crimp in Rufus's narcissism. He could no longer persuade himself he was going to get to everything he wanted to write before he himself had to toddle off. And since time had begun to press (Janice, for example, only <u>seemed</u> immortal), Rufus could now see where he might be useful to an unforeseeable future simply by getting some of the obvious materials in enough shape so some hypothetical historian might some fine day make something of them.

Usually at Lois and Janice's you weren't told in advance who the other comida guests might be. So there would be a rap on the distant front door, or the bell would ring and if Beta wasn't at a critical moment in her cooking she would go scurrying, or if Beta was occupied, Janice would pull herself up and go hobbling out. Even from the living room you could hear the bolt shoot back, loud as a rifle discharge, and then indistinct murmuring and pleasant laughter along the corridor and then at the glass doors would appear—perhaps--people you might not have met up with in a number of years.

Or in this case, a couple of months (Maryanne Fort) and almost thirty years (Maryanne's daughter Rennie, last seen by Rufus as a babe in Giles Fort's uneasy custody outside a lecture hall). When Rufus uncoiled himself from his chair and stood, Maryanne put out her hand and was pleasant. He felt he deserved it, having done her the favor of linking her up with Rosie Utrillo. The daughter was freshly bathed, frizzed-out hair still a little damp, and stolid, glum, or maybe just ill at ease because she was so new to the scene (though not really, he remembered, since Rennie had spent some of her early childhood in San Cristóbal and also out in Manantiales).

They settled in, Janice and Maryanne side by side on the couch, Rennie and Rufus in the chairs, Buster the male cat stretched out imperiously and disdainful atop his bookcase. Maryanne put her hand over on Janice's and Janice laid her other old arthritis-gnarled one on top. The smell of onions sizzling in hot cooking oil from the open kitchen on the other side of the room was entirely promising. Fresh juice *licuados* were offered, today a frothy piña one or dark red hibiscus. Booze was seldom seen at Lois and Janice's, unless someone brought a bottle of wine, which would be put on the table to consume with the food.

Maryanne and Janice fell to reminiscing about the earliest days, stories and bits Rufus knew well, so probably the ladies were bringing them forth for Rennie's benefit. How in the beginning Janice and Lois had a little adobe and tile house out almost a third of the way up Huitepec. It rented for five dollars a month, which meant poor as they were they could just keep it and leave their stuff when they had to go back to New York to earn money. There was never any doubt about the goal, though, Janice maintained. Never anything other than to live in Mexico as much of the time as they could manage.

"God, but how many trips did that take over the years?" Janice said. "Actually, I used to know. But I've forgotten. I did the driving and Lois navigated. And kvetched."

In New York, to save as much as possible they tried always to housesit friends' apartments, subletting only when they had to. Lois would go back to work as a substitute teacher, and Janice would pick up a job drawing out plans at some architectural firm. "And when we'd have enough so we could live here another year or two years, I'd quit and we'd come," she said.

Maryanne said, "In the 50s... Wasn't that a little scary, quitting?"

"Are you kidding? Quitting has always been my favorite thing."

Rennie came out of herself long enough for one short laugh.

According to Janice, getting Lois packed up for the trip was always a big hassle, no matter which direction they were going. "She was an artist, you know, and they are ditherers."

"And you? You're not an artist for some reason?"

Janice looked down. "I'm at least a mechanical-minded person," she said. "I'll go that far."

So what she had done eventually, she went on, was go out and get boxes, 28 of them all different sizes, and fit them in so they filled up the entire space of the trunk and the back seat of their beloved old Dodge sedan. Then she'd bring the boxes in and put them in the middle of the floor and let Lois futz about and get in everything she wanted to take with them this time.

"Tell about when you were popped at the border," Rufus said. "Rennie might like to hear that one."

"Oh." Janice had to think a minute. "Well, we had this friend in New York, Marsha, and Marsha got cancer. Bad. Painful. In her colon, poor thing. And we felt so sorry for her, and her darned doctor wouldn't give her enough painkillers because he was afraid she was going to get addicted to them. I mean, Marsha was dying, right?" Janice's face was suddenly contorted and fierce. Then it softened again. "Well down here in those days you could buy anything you might want over the counter, so Marsha called us and told us what she needed and we loaded up. And at Laredo the U.S. guys started pulling out the boxes and going through our stuff, which ordinarily they never did. Did somebody tip them off? I'll never know. But anyway at first we weren't even worried as I recall. We thought since the medications weren't for us...and since it was all legal in Mexico.... We were very naïve....

"'Whose pills are these?' this one mug wants to know. And Lois looks at me only a second and volunteers...which wasn't even quite true. I was the one who had bought them. But they handcuffed her and took her off to jail. I had no idea what to do, so I went and ate...some really greasy chile I couldn't finish... and then I called our friend Hal the lawyer in New York and he said he'd get right on it and make some phone calls. But that sounded to me like it might take a while, so I went down to where they had Lois in the basement of some federal building there and I demanded to see her and when they took me in and I saw her behind bars I demanded they lock me up too. With Lois, right there in the same cell. And they were like, 'What, lady? What?' and acting like I was a crazy person, but I told them quite firmly Mrs. Bloch was the woman I had come across from Mexico with and I meant to <u>be</u> with her and take half of whatever shit it was—I didn't use the word, actually, but something a little more polite— whatever it was they were planning on handing her. 'Whither thou goest' I told them, 'whither thou goest!' So then they really did think I was a complete nut case and maybe they were a little scared of me or at least a little ashamed of themselves for putting such a nice person as Lois in the hoosegow like that. And by then I had managed to dig out the scrips Marsha had collected in New York and sent down to us. I assumed these were bogus, but I waved 'em at the customs men and demanded they show me where it was written you couldn't have a U.S. prescription for Demerol filled in Mexico. And of course those pumpkins weren't capable of doing that, so they had to let Lois go."

"Did you get to keep Marsha's drugs for her?"

"What?" Janice seemed momentarily nonplussed, then turned belligerent. "Of course we did!"

In his own case, Rufus had expected the last period of his lover Javier's life to be a long spate of emergencies and intensive care stays. But Javier weakened and glided downhill, eventually sleeping 20 or so hours a day, and then died quite simply and quietly at home, never having been hospitalized for anything. Rufus was left armed with documents and prepared speeches about their partnership he never needed to use. But what about Janice the multiple times Lois was air-ambulanced to Houston? "And at Methodist Hospital when you guys would go there, did they ever hassle you or try to exclude you?" he asked.

Janice again seemed to draw a blank. "Why would they do that?"

'You and Janice being no kin of any sort?"

"No," Janice shook her head, "never any problem there I can recall."

He had to laugh at himself. Ask a stupid question. What nurse or doctor or hospital administrator in her or his right mind would even imagine trying to bar Janice from a consultation or a hospital room? Maybe the U.S. Customs agents had put out their mug shots and a general warning all over Texas: MAKE NO ATTEMPT TO FUCK WITH THESE TWO OLD BROADS.

Beta had come out behind them and laid the salad on the dining table. She spoke softly to Janice and Janice bade everyone to move across the room to eat. The guests were on their feet when a faint rapping on the French doors' glass startled them.

It was Patrick Durban, the young man with the International Red Cross who had rented Janice's little casita for the last couple of years. He had come only to say goodbye and hand over the keys, he said. Lean in his beltless, much-washed jeans, Patrick had blue blue eyes and hair so blond it was almost white. He was in his early 30s, and as Janice and Rufus had once discussed, so intent on radiating a sense of calm that it was almost impossible to tell anything about what his human desires might be. Though Rufus was no more than merely curious about the subject, he first thought Patrick was probably gay, or at least as they say 'questioning.' But Janice said oh no, there <u>was</u> a young lady in the picture, her name was Sheila, and while in two years she hadn't managed to make a visit to San Cristóbal, she and Patrick wrote each other regularly. And how did Janice know all that? Well, she said, Patrick got his mail in her box, and put his outgoing letters there too. And you feel free to review them? Rufus asked. Well, not the contents, Janice said, but the envelopes, sure. It's my mailbox, right?

Particular as Janice was, few of the renters of the casita had worked out as well as Patrick. He possessed a mix of stick-to-himself and need for company which meshed nicely with Janice's own. Out of season, as she so often claimed, she was perennially lonely for people and, seeing her lights still on, Patrick had gotten the habit of dropping in 'just to say hello' at the end of his own long days of doing good. She was going to miss him, Janice confessed to Rufus.

But now there wasn't really time for anything more than Patrick depositing his keys on the bookcase by the door as instructed and a brief hug, the tall young man and the stooped old lady. The other comida guest, the poet Evgenia Swift, was hurrying in, excusing herself for being so late as she came. Patrick blushed a bright pink and began apologizing for holding up the party.

"Go ahead and sit," Janice ordered and followed Patrick out toward the front door.

In Lois's day, there were often surprises and oohs and aahs when the main dish was laid on the table. But while all of Beta's cooking followed Lois's recipes to the letter--so much so that every taste in the meal recalled her--there were no more innovations. Chicken pieces stewed in a garlic broth, or fish filets with swiss chard, small oven-broiled potatoes or a rice pilaf, a loaf of homemade wheat bread on a board with the knife beside it. Janice liked to heap your plate with one of the items, then to encourage passing of the others. Seconds were always offered, especially to male guests, then Janice would pull the salad bowl down from its place at the far end of the table and portion out lettuce, cucumber, and tomato pieces onto people's plates. A small silver bowl of already made up oil-and-vinegar you dipped and dripped with a small silver spoon that was a souvenir of the 1939 New York World's Fair. Both the bowl and the spoon were secondary relics of Lois.

Being introduced to Rennie Fort, Evgenia said her
nickname was "Gini." But people like Rufus and Maryanne
who had known her a long time often slipped and still called
her "Evie," which she now professed to hate. ("Evie!' she would
say. 'Sounds like I should be leaping from ice floe to ice floe to
get across a freezing river.') She was tiny, fine-boned, darting
and pecking in style in both her eating and her conversation.
Having lived twenty-some years in San Cristóbal, Evie was full
of jaundiced opinion about other gringos in town. Today she
seemed intent on finding out what Janice had gotten from Petra
Hobbs and hubby Sandro for the two Lois paintings and the big
Lois transglow they had just bought. Janice of course was not
about to reveal any dollar or peso amount, but did say that that
new husband of Petra's was a real buttinsky and certainly drove
a hard bargain.

Evie Swift nodded emphatically, as though this confirmed
long-hatching suspicions of hers.

Rufus could imagine why Sandro might take a jaundiced
view of Lois's art. Much of it had fallen into disrepair. The
chronic damp of SanCris had bestowed mildew on the
paintings, some of the transglow boxes were coming unglued,
and everything needed professional cleaning. Evie espoused
the belief that Lois was going to be discovered posthumously
and so thought the collection should be held together against a
possible sale to a single benefactor or a prominent gallery. And
in fact though the details remained cloudy, she had a candidate.
Na Bolom. The well-known guest house and museum of the
Danish archeologist Frans Blom and his wife Gertrudis Duby

had just now, six years after Trudi's death, passed into the hands of a wealthy Mexico City family with roots in San Cristóbal. They had grand plans for the old place to be brightened up and made a super A-list tourist destination. They also wanted Na Bolom to become the repository for the work of the best artists of Chiapas, Mexican and from elsewhere. And Evie, who claimed to have once interned with the hottest of Madison Avenue dealers, had convinced them to hire her part-time to begin making acquisitions.

Evie claimed a lot, held her life together through self-promotion. The four corners of her business card read PHOTO-JOURNALIST/POET/ EDITOR/EXPERT. Janice had faith in her. She had turned Lois's diaries over to see if there wasn't some kind of book Evie could make out of Lois's thoughts about art over the years.

After salad there usually came a little dish of chopped fresh fruit and then Beta would place before Janice a tray with cups and a Thermos and an array of teas in little metal canisters and paper boxes for guests to choose from. Coffee was offered as well, but since it had to be made separately it took a little courage to ask for it. (Rufus had this courage.) Then store-bought cake, sometimes a little past fresh but always thickly iced, and/or cookies, and finally the hostess calling for Beta to bring particular different chocolates from the hoard in the little storeroom behind the refrigerator.

The jolly encouraging way Janice doled out the sweets led to a kind of further loosening in the atmosphere at the table that wine might otherwise have brought on. Focusing on silent, glum Rennie Fort, Evie undertook to tell a story Rufus already knew about a lady anthropologist from the early days. Cleaning out her closets and drawers at home in the States, this woman found a lot of good used clothes and underwear so she brought the whole lot with her Chiapas to give away to her Indian friends. "Well," Evie said, "I don't know—have you been to Chamula yet?"

Rennie looked to her mother. "I don't think so. We were in the village yesterday."

"Ah, but that was your mother's village, right? Manantiales. The point here is that Chamula is cold country and they raise sheep."

"As they do in Manantiales," Maryanne said softly.

Evie frowned at the interruption. "Well whatever," she said. "The point is that to keep their flocks from eating everything, especially when they're passing through someone else's property, the Chamula women weave little muzzles to put on them. It's fun to see. But this poor lady anthropologist! The next time she went out there for a fiesta or whatever something familiar caught her eye. Seems the ladies who'd been given her old brassieres cut them in two and were using the cups and straps for sheep muzzles!"

There was some amusement around the table, and then Maryanne Fort said, "That was me in fact."

"Oh." Evie sniffed. Rufus thought she was going to apologize, but instead she looked away for a moment, then back at Maryanne, and said evenly, "I never knew exactly who it was."

Ordinarily after comida they would have returned to the chairs and the couch, but today Evie announced she had an appointment. Rufus had one too, he was to be at Na Bolom at four-thirty, so the whole group began moving along toward the front of the house. Rennie needed the bathroom, which stood between Lois's bedroom and Janice's and also had a door on the corridor. When she emerged, Janice suggested that since the casita was for the moment unoccupied perhaps they'd like to see what she'd done with it.

In all the years he had been coming to San Cristóbal, Rufus had never been in the casita. There were two sizeable rooms. The living room-study had a large plain polished wood desk in front of a window which looked out on a walled brick patio and garden, leather sling chairs from Yucatán drawn up toward an open fireplace and behind a four-burner stove, sink, and work counter kitchen. The bedroom was of equal size with a tiled bathroom off it. It was easy to see how the precise, organization-minded soul who would fill her car with 28 cardboard boxes had been at work here too. Though there were no closets, floor-to-ceiling mahogany shelving had been set into the adobe walls in a number of places, entirely convenient for clothes, books, towels, cooking equipment, food.

On expanses of white-washed wall in the main rooms Janice had placed big abstractions by Lois. Both rooms had skylights. The glow they gave off on a clouded-in afternoon like this picked up and intensified Lois's already strong colors. Even in the main house, Rufus had never seen Lois's paintings displayed so attractively. Yet no one commented on them until they were all about to go out, when in a low, confidential voice Janice said to Rennie, "The pictures don't <u>have</u> to be here. I'd take them down if the renter didn't want them."

Rennie looked up again at the piece over the mantel, an enlarged version of an Indian cross built up and made to look almost 3-D by the application of impasto squares, dark blue at the corners going to bright white yellows at the center. "Who wouldn't want these?" Rennie said, and she trailed off back into the bedroom to take a second look at the Lois there. Janice went stumping along in after her. Silence, an echoing silence from the bedroom, the others waiting. Then Rennie and Janice emerged and the general progress toward the front door resumed.

"<u>You're</u> an artist I hear."

Rennie said, "Not really."

"But you've had training, right?" Janice asked. "Classes?"

Rennie shook her head, her frizz bobbing freely. Then admitted, "Well, some maybe. Mostly about how to teach art to kids, though."

"But still," Janice said, "you paint."

"I have. A little."

"I don't suppose you have anything with you."

Rennie laughed, embarrassed. "I'd have to look. Maybe a couple colored pencil sketches. And I did have a couple postcards made up one time."

The entrance to the casita was only forty or so feet down the sidewalk from the door to the main house. Though the barrio of Cerrillo was no longer as poor as it had been when Janice and Lois moved there, some families still sold bootleg liquor to Indians, so by the end of the day there were often teenage boy drunks swaying in the street, barely on their feet, frequently with large pee stains down their pantslegs. They panhandled some, but they were usually too wasted to be aggressive about it. Today the gringos had to get around a man sprawled asleep up against Janice's wall. Several lean neighborhood dogs stood aside, waiting to get back to sniffing at his raggedy clothes.

At the door, even as Evie Swift started into her thanks and goodbyes, Janice seemed unwilling to let any of them go. When Evie paused, she said, "You know, I think you were away when we placed Lois's stone, weren't you?"

"Yes, I was in Tuxtla...or was it Mexico City?"

"Well don't you want to come down and see how it came out?" Turning to Rufus and Maryanne, she said, "And you too? Come along." Janice acted as though it was a lovely treat she was offering.

Inside, she laid her cane against a bench and asked Rennie for her arm and the whole little group trooped through and out into the garden, then down to the foot of the property where there was a big shady tree near the fence. Dirt had been mounded up around the tree's base, outlined by a perfect circle of stones, and impatiens planted. In the midst of the flowers stood a foot-and-a-half high piece of sparkly white granite, sheared off on one side. Lois's name, birth date and death date, and a kind of Celtic-looking geometric flower border, nothing more. Rufus knew the stone carver, a tiny 80-year-old with flowing white hair and grossly enlarged knuckles who kept a dusty little workshop four or five blocks from Janice's. Rufus was fairly sure Don Ángel did not know how to read, or at least didn't know very well. He never questioned anything about a text or made a correction. What you printed out for him was exactly what he carved, upper and lower cases freely mixed.

They stood a long moment gazing down. Then Evie said, "Very nice, Janice. Simple, appropriate."

"Mine's over there," Janice said, "in case any of you should need to know." She pointed out a similar-sized piece of what looked like the same stone over against the fence, half obscured by weeds, cast-off looking.

"Oh," said Evie, "but not for a long time, Janice."

"You think? I'm thinking maybe not so much longer."

The old lady took Rennie's arm again and started back up, Evie trucking after them. Rufus and Maryanne stayed a bit, regarding the place where Lois's ashes were buried. When they turned and began to follow, Janice and Rennie were stopped at the brow of the hill, heads bent together in conversation.

"Do you see what I see?" Rufus asked.

"You mean the seduction?" Maryanne laughed. "Yes—"

Their old friends all agreed. While Lois was alive she was the one who drew the people she and Janice wanted into their web. But it turned out that all along Janice was watching and learning, and when Lois died she stepped up and took over the task. And proved just as good at it—or even better—than her partner had been.

"—but Rennie's a bit of a hard sell you know."

"You think she'll be able to resist?"

"Well, everything she let on to Janice about her ambitions was prevarication. 'Some classes?' She has an MFA in painting, you know. And the training to become a children's art teacher thing? Bogus. A fall-back position during one of a series of crises about whether Rennie could ever make it as a 'real' artist or not."

"Why that worry? If you want to be an artist, don't you just do the work and try not to think about whether you're 'for real' or not?"

"Certainly from what we can tell that was Lois's way."

"And Janice's."

"Indeed. But then neither of them had their own father pontificating that—" and here Maryanne's voice deepened in imitation of Giles's "—it is unlikely there's much possibility in our genes or whatever that any Fort will turn out to be truly artistic.'"

"So did Giles think that you all were blessed only with the social sciences gene?"

"If that were so, why didn't any of our kids follow in our footsteps? But I shouldn't be disloyal. Giles pushed that on the older ones, but by the time Rennie came along he'd given it up. He doted on her, you know. So her doubts about herself must have come from somewhere else."

"Did you know the Newberry has asked if I'd do Giles's papers?"

"No." Maryanne hesitated. "What does that mean? 'Do' his papers."

"Put them in order, you know, make them into an archive."

"Oh."

"Is that a problem?"

"No." She laughed it off, then looked hard at Rufus. "A bit of a surprise is all. I just assumed that putting Giles' things in order was a task I'd have to do myself at some point. Or at least that they would consult with me about who should do it."

"I'm sure they just missed a step by coming to me first. If you'd rather—"

"No, no," she touched his arm. "You knew Giles, I'm sure you'll do a bang-up job. And in fact it relieves me of some work, doesn't it?"

Now the others were waiting for them. Four o'clock exactly on Rufus's watch. Again Evie started into her goodbyes. But Janice stopped her, asked her to wait just a minute, and hobbled off into the bathroom. Maryanne asked Rennie, "What were you and Janice saying?"

"Oh. She was telling me about how the neighbors were in the beginning, always calling Lois the *Señora Bloch* because she had been married and Janice the *Señorita Metz* and either never suspecting they were a couple or at least much too discreet ever to let on that they knew—"

"But?"

"I guess it's all changed. She says now the kids look for tiny stones and drop them in the front door keyhole and screw up the lock so she has to take it apart to get the stones out and then put the whole thing back together again. Do you think that could be true, Mom?"

"I don't know why I'd doubt it."

"Not just old lady paranoia stuff?"

"Well--"

They were talking now almost in whispers.

"She invited me to live in the casita."

"What did you say?"

"I said oh no thanks, I was only going to be here for a month at the most."

"Honey, that's an offer I wouldn't have refused."

"Really?"

"Janice doesn't offer it to just anybody you know."

"She said she thought I could be a help to her going over her photographs, since Rufus was leaving soon."

They could hear the toilet flush, there was a pause and Janice came out and led her guests out to the front door.

In the street, Evie Swift still hung on. She asked Rennie, "Did you notice the bathrobes?"

"No, where?"

"On the bathroom door into Lois's room there's a nice frilly one—it's still there—and on Janice's door an L.L. Bean men's in green plaid."

"Oh." Rennie looked to her mother, apparently confused, then back. "And?"

"It's the famous butch-femme aesthetic at work, right?"

"I'm sorry, I don't know what you're talking about."

"No? Has all that gone out of fashion so quickly? The bathrobes are symbols Lois and Janice put up to tell us which of them was the man and which one the woman."

"Oh," Rennie said again.

Evie gave her laugh, which was meant to tinkle, but sounded strangely like driveway gravel crunching in the night.

What Rufus saw in Rennie was a look of distaste, although it may have only been indifference or embarrassment.

Janice had loosened up considerably since Lois's death, but in earlier days both women treated their being lovers as a secret made available only to dear friends and not to be mentioned by anyone unless they themselves chose to. Why would Evie treat their hanging their robes out like flags for those with eyes to see as something skuzzy? To Rufus it had always seemed only entirely endearing.

⬥

That evening when he came back to Janice's for a book she had promised to lend him, Rufus noticed a faint glow along the top of the casita wall.

"Did we leave lights on?" he asked. "Shall I go over and turn them off?"

"No," said Janice, "that's Rennie. She's getting settled in."

"She changed her mind then."

"She did. Came back an hour after you left with her mother and said she'd be pleased if I'd rent her the casita, even if it was only for a little while."

"And you said …?"

"I said, 'Well then, why don't you just go along down to your hotel and get your stuff, OK?'"

"And she did."

"She did." Then Janice said, "Come, sit."

Rufus pulled two chairs up closer to the fire and they turned their backs on the cold of the evening. The wood readily available for sale in San Cristóbal is pine, and though conveniently split into small, short sticks, it burns very fast. But Janice and Lois had planned the renovation of the house they bought in the Sixties with great care, Janice drawing up every detail for the masons and the carpenters to follow, so the shallow, domed-oven-style fireplace she had designed retained heat and kept even pine coals breathing for a long time.

Both women had always feasted on gossip, demanding whatever you brought up front. Since Lois's death, Janice's hunger for the "juicy stuff" as she called it had only increased. Coming and going as Rufus did, and without any large set of San Cristóbal sources that didn't overlap with hers, he was often a disappointment to her. "<u>YOU</u>!" she charged him once, "you're up on all the news…of 30 years ago!"

A fitting indictment against an historian, he thought. If that was what he really was.

In the absence of fresh fodder, they ruminated on the old. Though it was actually history of a sort they were talking, gringos and other foreigners who passed through Chiapas was not a story Rufus felt any responsibility for, so he could float just as libidinously through the eras as Janice did. The way their conversations ran reminded him of summer nights in his childhood, his North Carolina aunts and his grandmother out on the porch, the metal chairs that rocked just a little, the women's genealogical recitations—many of which little Rufus already had memorized—and then the sudden sharp turn of the narrative of a cousin or second cousin he had never met into a divorce or being sent home from the university for drinking, or a scandal that must have been much worse because the ladies never named it directly and even at six or seven he could tell he wasn't supposed to ask any more about it.

With age Janice's judgments about people had become fixed, not subject to revision even if you came before her with striking new evidence. A number of her opinions Rufus thought knee-jerk or just dead wrong.

About Aaron Levine, for example. A medical doctor now deceased, Aaron lived the last fifteen years of his life first in San Cristóbal and then in Comitán, a town two hours down the mountains toward Guatemala in a more temperate zone. Rufus was a little put out with himself, though not ashamed, about claiming he'd now become an historian to Maryanne Fort. The way gossip ran in SanCris, it was likely she would have learned soon enough he'd put aside history the last three summers in order track the progress of AIDS in Chiapas and had been working with Aaron Levine on a small project trying to learn about bisexual men in Comitán. Since he was both a doctor and an outsider, a certain number of men in town had trusted Aaron enough to share confidences about their *sub rosa* sexual practices. But when Aaron spoke with some of the married fellows about being interviewed, none of them was willing to meet Rufus. What if word about them got out? They reminded the *simpatico* gringo doctor that Comitán was a very closed little place full of tattle-tales and vipers.

When Rufus mentioned how fond he had been of Aaron, Janice agreed. "They can tar and feather away as they like, but to my mind there was nothing wrong with Aaron except that he wasn't as good a doctor as he thought he was."

Though Rufus knew what would come next, he said, "What do you mean, Janice?"

Though both Janice and Lois hated illness, they loved to put their faith in doctors and then to find them wanting and write them off. Nearly every physician in San Cristóbal had been their medical miracle man at one time or another, but if you asked Janice today who to go to, she would tell you every last one of them was a quack and might well send you off to somewhere on the edge of town where the "doctor" turned out to be really only a chiropractor or podiatrist with an office so dingy you couldn't make out much in the diplomas on the wall behind his head. Aaron and Janice and Lois, all three refugees in some sense from the red-baiting of the 1950s, cared a great deal for one another. So Aaron's fall from favor in medical matters had taken the ladies a good while. Rufus knew if he asked Janice would tell him in no uncertain terms that Aaron's luring her down to Comitán when she broke her hip and the hard cast they put her in had been a near-fatal mistakes. The fact that the thing, solid plaster from waist to toes, <u>worked</u> on a woman then already in her eighties did not dissuade her. Janice had a touching belief in her body's ability to heal more or less instantly and had never forgiven Aaron for the eight tedious weeks she spent immobilized in the clunky thing.

Though it no longer mattered, Janice continued to worry the issue of the dietary habits of a man of sixty who was a stomach cancer survivor. Aaron himself admitted he tried to stay with the fruit salads he made on the weekend, but eating right was a battle he too often lost. What he longed for—what he <u>needed</u> in some way—was the food of his youth, which he found at Sam's Club in Tuxtla. Herring in cream sauce, big vats of sour cream, farmers cheese or ricotta, sausages, a whole panoply of prepared meats, even deadly bottled pepperoncini. The noodle kugel he brought sometimes to Lois and Janice's was so rich Lois claimed she didn't sleep a wink afterwards.

"So I would ask her, 'Is that why you always have seconds, Sweetie?'" Janice said. She sighed, thought. "Aaron," she said, "he had all those things wrong with him, the diverticulitis, all that crummy stuff. So what was with him? He was a doctor. Did he not want to live?"

"I don't think it's that," Rufus said. "Aaron definitely wanted life."

Janice stared at him, finally said, "What then? Was he not capable of some self-control?"

"What if he weren't?" said Rufus.

Janice looked down at her gnarled old hands, sighed.

"Janice?" Rufus pursued her a little. "You and I both know about dieting don't we? Remember what you told me once?"

"No."

"You said you thought lifetime you had lost over 500 pounds."

She was laughing again. "I said that? Well it must be true then." Then she said, "What I can't understand about Aaron was all that about the waiters at the Alhambra."

The Alhambra was one of the biggest hotels in town, usually near full occupancy with large groups of one- or two-night European tourists. The enterprise belonged to a woman named Greta Contreras, gotten as the settlement in her divorce from the eldest son of a Chiapas landowning family. By carefully preserving an accent in both English and Spanish, Greta emphasized her Russian ancestry, although people said she was a much larger percent German than she admitted and the Russian was really only a sprinkling. It was Greta who had poured the little drops of poison about Aaron and her waiters into Janice's ear.

"You know when he had to be up here on business two days in a row Aaron usually stayed there at the Alhambra. And he'd take that one really expensive room, what Greta calls the 'suite.'"

"Yes?"

"Well, it has a hottub you know, and the waiters and the bellboys say Aaron would invite them up to join him for a soak."

"Not all of them together?" Rufus feigned concern.

"No," said Janice. "One at a time I suppose."

"And did any of them ever take Aaron up on the offer?"

She laughed a little. "That I don't know. Not reported. So I take it you're not surprised."

"Some of those guys at the Alhambra are pretty good-looking, you know."

"I've not noticed."

"Well they are. I'll vouch for it."

Silence.

After a bit, he went on, "What's at issue here, Janice? Certainly it's not a shock to you that a person might have—what shall we call it this time?—a certain <u>fluidity</u> in his sexual interests?"

"No, of course not. But Aaron...couldn't he be more discreet?"

"Than to invite a handsome hotel waiter up to share a hottub after a long day on his feet? It's the waiter who lacks discretion, isn't it? Ratting Aaron out to his boss?"

Janice had to laugh. "I suppose," she said. But she couldn't let it go at that. "It's that business of appetites, isn't it? Aaron not in control of himself, that's what surprises me."

Rufus decided to let the matter lie. There would, after all, be no convincing Janice of anything different once her mind was made up.

He didn't love the old girl any less. Amazing in her way for a woman her age. Since Lois's death she had begun coming out to him more and more. Stories about girlfriends back in the 40s before Lois and how when the Party told her she had to drop them Janice told them to go fly a kite, her personal life was her personal life. And about how she, Janice, for years and years had to put up with the hovering of Laurie, the woman so in love with Lois she pulled up stakes in New York and trailed them all the way to San Cristóbal. Janice managed to get this Laurie to stand down and retreat as far as Oaxaca for some time with only occasional visits to Chiapas. But next to their own house Lois and Janice also owned the much smaller *casita*, so when Laurie took somewhat mysteriously ill Janice had to give in and allow her rival to come and rent the smaller place.

One sunny but chill afternoon as she was seeing Rufus along the corridor toward her front door, Janice stopped dead and indicated the morning glory covered wall on the far side of her patio with the tip of her cane. "See that?"

"Yes, sure."

"I had it built. That medical business of Laurie's whatever it was supposed to be didn't get her down half as much you'd think it would. It seemed like every time I left the house she was skipping across over here to visit with Lois. So I figured I better put a stop to that."

Rufus laughed. "You walled her out."

"Well at least I made it so she had to come around to the front door and ring the bell like any decent person, yes."

So it was not as though Janice did not understand the mess that almost inevitably comes in the same package with love (or sex, if you'd rather). But would she necessarily have a feeling for the built-up needs of a senior guy who lived with no expectation of the comfort of a softly shushing warm body of either sex next to him in the night? Male horniness. Different from the female variety, no? So strong when it comes on you, so poignant, consuming all thought. <u>A typhoon! A hurricane is moving toward Mahagonny!</u> But also passing quickly, whether there's an orgasm in the process or not. All the jokes about men being ruled by their dicks are true enough, but in the end may not say much about the character of the individual fellow, for example one who sometimes, when he's away from home and finished with his lonely supper, may interpret (or misinterpret) a small kindness or a look in the waiter's eye while he's laying out the tip and so wonders could there be something more, some permission, some equivalent pang of desire being expressed? Which might lead to an invitation to the tub and then the big bed waiting upstairs…

Janice cocked her head up as though she heard something in the corridor. But no. "It couldn't take much to unpack one suitcase, could it?" she said. "I told the young lady she should come over, we'd have a nice fire. What do you think? Maybe she's shy. Why don't you go, Rufus, and knock on her door. Tell her we can have some chocolate too."

Her friends knew how much Janice loved the stuff, so they brought it to her, European, American, bars, bricks, soft centers, chocolate-coated toffees, always the best stuff. Over time the size of her stash in the cupboard behind the refrigerator grew to be enormous. Eating chocolate with Janice was in a way like a visit to Tiffany. She laid out various things, you considered, you chose, you reported on what you'd tried, Janice judged her own piece, encouraged you to have another. In the process, a good deal of candy could be consumed, although always under the rubric of 'just one more,' or 'we're really only tasting here, aren't we?'

CB

With Rennie ensconced at Janice's and having learned the way to the market to buy herself some fruit and vegetables and eggs, rather suddenly Maryanne began to think it time for her to go home. Nothing urgent, although she did look forward to finding a moment alone in Helen's kitchen so she could duck down and retrieve Giles's ashes from the canning supplies cupboard. What a stupid idea that had been! Whatever state of mind led her to make that drop-off had passed, thank goodness! She did not like admitting in the end of February that she had been so off her game in the beginning of the same short month, but that seemed to be the case.

She felt obligated to go to Manantiales and tell Losha she was leaving. In a chance meeting with Señor Utrillo on the street he said he and Rosie would be making a trip out there the next day, so Maryanne was able to hitch a ride with them. It was very quiet in the village center, for some reason neither of the cantinas was casting the usual Mexican radio music into the humid air. So quiet you could hear the tinkling sounds of steel-string harps being stroked and faint voices chanting down in the direction of the Ermita. But Maryanne did not see any people down there.

She started up the long incline to Losha's, but about a hundred yards on she came upon the girl Marta on her way down. Her grandmother was not home, the girl told her, she was washing clothes. Would Maryanne want to go visit her there? Of course, Maryanne said.

Instead of leading her to the river, Marta led Maryanne into an enclosed courtyard beside the Ermita. There they found Losha on her knees in the middle of a good-sized crowd. The women around her, most of them quite young, had long barge-shaped wooden basins filled with sudsy water and clothing. A number of the saint figures from inside the chapel had been brought out in the sun to watch while some of their vestments were washed. Each of them had big boxes of clothing to choose from, so they were already gowned in other of their things.

An early mistake of the anthropologists had been to believe the religious cargos were held only by men, while in fact they involved duties—and prestige and fun—for wives and families as well. In this case, the male cargo-holders stood about, smoking and joshing one another. Everyone was decked out in ceremonial finery, short black wool tunics, ribboned hats and coin necklaces for the men, the women in their best embroidered blouses, hair precisely combed and pulled back and braided with ribbons. As soon as she was informed Maryanne was there, Losha called for her to come and sit beside her. The old lady was in charge of the operation, giving orders to the men to come empty the basins and refill them with fresh water, ordering up a new round of drinks. The others were nicely tipsy and several of the women made it their business to get Maryanne to join them and drink up.

She didn't especially want to get drunk. She had a long list of things to do in SanCris tomorrow, Janice's birthday the next day, then two days later in the afternoon Lupe's cab to Tuxtla to catch her plane. But the atmosphere in the courtyard attracted and lulled her. Everyone was so attentive to the task, serious and yet happy and joking at the same time. When the saints' clothes had been rinsed a number of times and by dipping her finger over and over into it and then tasting Losha deemed the wash water was coming entirely clear, she told the cargo-holders now they should drink the last of it. What? They had never heard of that. Oh yes, Losha maintained, that was how it was done in the old days, and if the custom had lapsed that was not her fault. The thought of drinking the wash water seemed to make the crowd even more giddy than multiple rounds of colorless aguardiente had. Big glasses were brought and filled and people looked down into them a long moment and some prayed in low voices and crossed themselves several times before toasting others and drinking.

"I'm going, my mother," Maryanne whispered.

"To San Cristóbal? You just arrived."

"No, back to my own country."

"Huh!   Well—" Losha's sightless eyes were rheumy, yellowed, likely the required drinking taking its toll. "Well then, my daughter, go on. But don't die along the road."

It was an older formulation, less often used these days. It made Maryanne laugh to hear it again. "I won't," she promised.

At four that afternoon, back in San Cristóbal, Maryanne was due to drop in to bid goodbye to Petra Hobbes and Sandro the new husband. Though Petra was not actively put out with Maryanne, she had been complaining about how this stay hadn't given them much good time together, what with her old friend out in the field for weeks on end.

Maryanne knocked and waited and knocked again, but no one came to the door. It was a dry, sunny afternoon, traffic on the street picking up again after the midday lull. She still felt a little woozy from the drinks she'd consumed in Manantiales, but she was also calm. After Maryanne knocked a third time, she picked up some hollow shuffling inside, and at last Miguel, the older Chamula gentleman who watched after Petra's house, undid the bolts and cracked the door enough at least for Maryanne to see his nose and one eye.

"The *señores* aren't at home," he said.

"Will they be back?"

"I don't know, *Señora*."

"I'm expected. May I come in and wait?"

Miguel did not move to open the door any farther.

"Miguelito? You know me, don't you?"

He nodded.

"Well may I come in then?"

Finally Miguel swung the door back enough for her to squeeze in. She was led up into the patio and offered a seat on one of the benches. The main rooms of the house were all shut up. By the big window Petra had had installed in the sala, a stepladder leaned against the wall and overhead nailed at one end dangled a curved length of wire with a loop in the loose end. Maryanne assumed they were about to hang the Lois transglow Janice had sold Petra.

It was ten minutes before her old friend came hurrying in, a kind of red beanie or beret jammed down on her head, followed more slowly by tall Sandro, who was sporting a walking stick. He had on a tailored jacket and gray pants with a faint stripe to them and an ascot puffing from the open collar of his shirt. Apologies all around, tea offered ("Miguel will you put water on, I need to wash my hands"), doors flung open, and they made a move in to the couches by the fireplace in the living room.

"I'm sorry we're in such a flurry," Petra said once they were settled, "but we went to <u>try</u> at least to eat something to calm us down."

"Not that we were very successful at <u>that</u>, my dear," said Sandro, who remained standing behind his wife.

Pleased for her longtime lady pal to find someone after the previous husband checked out, Maryanne had never noticed what an odd couple Petra and Sandro made, she squat, energetic, big-hearted and with her ever-beautiful face, he with his Euro sneer and his wardrobe of what looked like faded versions of men's magazine clothes of the 1920s and 30s.

Petra dug around in her purse and came up waving an embroidered napkin. "Oh, look! From the restaurant. I'll have to take it back. They'll think I stole it."

"Where did you go?"

"The Jobel," Sandro said, "only because it's so near. Impossibly phony though it may be."

The place in question <u>was</u> entirely hokey, the waiters ladino boys costumed as Indians, two old men whacking the life out of a marimba so loud you couldn't hold a conversation. But since Sandro was still a relative newcomer to the scene, it was a little off-putting to hear him pronouncing so assuredly on questions of authenticity.

"Tell me what's happened," Maryanne said.

"Oh, we've had an awful shock," said Petra. She frowned a big sad pouty clown frown. "Just now, a couple of hours ago. And a scene too, although it was pretty much a scene in absentia."

"How was that?"

"We came in from Teopisca about two and at first thought we'd been robbed. Both of Lois's paintings and her transglow were <u>gone</u>!"

"Well my dear, we <u>were</u> robbed...in effect," Sandro said.

"But I'm confused. What was it really?"

"It seems Janice came to the door with two men—one of them was that gardener of hers--and Miguel opened up for her and she marched right in and they took everything down off the walls and carted them right out to Janice's car and off they went."

"Any idea what that was all about?"

"Oh yes. She left our check with Miguel torn into little pieces, and a note."

"Would you like me to bring it, my dear?" Sandro said.

"No, that's all right. Don't. Janice claims she has finally become aware of what the 'real' value of Lois's work is and that we were out to cheat her."

"But that's silly. You—"

"Of course it's silly," Petra said.

"You gave her what she asked in the first place, didn't you?"

Miguel came in with the tea on a tray, set it on the low table in front of Petra and padded away. Petra poured and handed round the cups, her hand so shaky the cups danced and rattled in their saucers.

Sandro took his, sipped, swallowed. He drew his cheeks in, which made his long face even longer. "I negotiated a reasonable price with that woman, yes. And there was maneuvering of course, although not an excessive amount. When you're talking about art, you are necessarily bound to talk about value as well."

"But now she says we beat her down and took advantage of her," Petra added. "And that we lack any respect at all for Lois and for her work."

"Ha!" Sandro said. "How crazy is that? I ask you. Why would you put good money out for an object if you didn't like it? The woman is nuts! Or senile, or both."

Petra lowered her head, dragged a little handkerchief out of her purse and began to sniffle into it. "And the main reason

I <u>wanted</u> those darn things was because I loved Lois so much. And Janice too. To have a little piece of them. What good times we had together in the old days. Isn't that true?"

"Oh yes," Maryanne agreed, "indeed."

"Well I personally see no reason to have anything further to do with that bitch," Sandro announced. "She has certainly made herself persona non grata with me. This is one house whose door is closed to her."

"Oh Sandro—" Petra looked miserable, "—please don't say things like that."

In his agitation, Sandro had begun stalking back and forth behind the couch. "No, no way, my dear. It's hardly about me, you know. I could care less! It's about you and her treatment of you. The offense to me is nothing, I am not of that woman's world. But the offense to you—<u>and</u> to that ancient friendship you invoke—is not to be overlooked."

Maryanne got up and came across and sat next to Petra and put an arm around her. The poor little woman was shaking all over now, and Maryanne herself began to feel so sad it seemed as though Petra's grief was flowing right across into her and filling her body too.

෫

These days Janice's birthday was an occasion which reflected a party she herself had started to celebrate her darling Lois when they first came to Mexico in the '50s and were making do on very little money. In the late afternoon of the day before her sweetie's birthday, Janice would go to the market when the stands were closing down and buy up cut flowers the vendors didn't think worth setting out another morning. These she put in every kind of container she could find and then hid in the bodega of the house they rented in those days. At dawn she would bring the flowers in and station them all around the living room and then she would make coffee and the people she had invited would sneak into the house. At a quarter to seven, the usual time for Janice to go wake up her love, she would call in and soon Lois would emerge from her room in her robe and nightie and everyone would cry 'Feliz cumpleaños!' and Lois would feign surprise and then there would be coffee and sweet rolls and warmed-up tamales prepared by the lady down the road. Nowadays her admirers made the same party for Janice. Beta arrived when it was still dark to let in the guests with their bouquets and Janice was the one who had to wait in her bedroom and listen to them whispering and bickering over where to put which vase and forgetting and speaking up and then shushing each other like children. No frilly bathrobe for Janice, however, or even the L.L. Bean plaid number. She came out in her worn old slacks and a shirt with her hair wet-combed and made no pretense of having just woken up, although for the sake of her fans she would feign some surprise at their being there, and then pleasure about the huge number of flowers.

Eighty-nine this time around. At the event itself, Rufus stood a little out the hubbub half-hidden by several cans of glads, drinking his coffee and eyeing the crowd hovering about the old girl in her usual place at the end of the couch. Knowing perfectly well all their connections to Janice and most of their connections to one another left him somewhat jaundiced about the motives that brought many of them around. Some of his sourness he recognized as jealousy. Who loved Janice best? He himself for sure, him and poor Aaron Levine. Some of the others present probably also loved her, but there were many false courtiers present as well, there to be seen, counted, Janice's birthday a kind of mustering of the militia or showing of the flag for the foreign colony and associate locals. People who came mostly to make sure no one badmouthed them, at least not at Janice's birthday <u>this</u> year.

In the old days (how many of his sentences was he beginning that way? or with 'Nowadays'? maybe better ration himself some). Start again: It used to be that to be friends with Janice and Lois you had to sign on at least implicitly to two basic premises. First, to a belief in their seriousness, Lois about her painting and Janice about her photography. And second, you had to believe as the critical fact about their relationship that there were two women who in middle age had thrown up convention, everything, and moved to Mexico in order to be together forever and ever. Until death did them part...

As it now had done, at least to the more literal-minded.

Since Lois's departure Janice had let things slip, no longer administered the old loyalty test. So now there were people in the room—if asked to play Inquisitor, Rufus would gladly finger them—who held with neither of the great articles of faith. For example, the poet Evie Swift (a.k.a. these days "Gini" if you wanted to humor her). In Evie's version of the two women's story

Lois's motivation had been to get away from an excruciatingly boring wimp of a husband and Janice's to duck out of the States because someone had named her—quite correctly—as a Communist.

The truth was that Janice (or Janice and the hovering shade of Lois) had lived long enough to become a tourist attraction. There was video on Youtube of Janice describing a trip into the Lacandón jungle with Trudi Blom. And in certain mostly left and mostly sapphic circles in Manhattan if you had visited SanCris without taking the two-day tour into liberated territory to eat beans with the Zapatistas and hadn't gone to drink tea with Janice your trip would be considered, if not a bust, at least lacking in authenticity.

Closest in around the Old One now, allowing others only brief audience with her, were the members of what Rufus called the Teutonic Mafia. No one else seemed to have noticed the minor irony that in recent years the old Jewish Red had been shanghaied by three German ladies. As Janice began to need more help—and, when her gringo friends were not in town, more company—it seemed logical that Greta, the owner of the Hotel Alhambra, would pitch in. She had known Lois and Janice so many years. Rufus also had faith in Hannah Seiden, a warm, short-haired accountant in early middle age divorced from her Mexican husband who had volunteered to make out the checks for Janice's regular monthly bills and to keep her books balanced. The oddity in the triumvirate was the artist Mitzi (no last name, apparently), who had two shops in town, both called "*La Mágica de Mitzi*." The magic Mitzi generated was mostly simply-drawn little boys and girls with apple-red cheeks and big smiles. They appeared on coffee mugs and in Mitzi-signed posters holding hands to make a circle around a stylized globe and bring about world peace and an end to ecological degradation, a goal to be accomplished through a donation of some unstipulated percentage of the profit from the sale of the poster itself. Her hottest items, however, were Mitzi-designed apple-cheeked ragdolls sewn together by indigenous women working into the night by kerosene lamp light and paid per piece less than a quarter of the item's retail price. Janice herself would only allow that Mitzi's products were somewhat kitschy. However, if you said no, they were better described as godawful, her eyes would light up but she would twist a pretend key to her lips to put a lock on them. Broad-faced, big-hipped Mitzi had won Janice's loyalty by looking in on her two or three times a week on her way to or from her shops, often bringing a loaf of multi-grain bread from the Mother Earth or the Casa de Pan or a container of locally-cultured yogurt.

Maryanne was glad to see Rennie had found herself a little niche for herself helping Beta with plates and glasses coming off the table and putting them out again washed and dried. She herself had been cornered a little by large Rufus Bright. Maryanne hated having to lie, disliked even the little fibs of social convenience, so she was glad when Rufus asked did she know whether Petra Hobbs had shown up yet and she could say no. And didn't need to add how unlikely it was that Petra would be putting in an appearance anytime soon.

"It's all so changed, isn't it?" Rufus asked, meaning she imagined San Cristóbal itself.

Maryanne said, "One thing I still find heartwarming though, is how, just like Mexicans, the resident gringos remain willing to fall out of their schedules."

Rufus laughed. "It's atavistic, isn't it? 'What? You've never seen the Carlos Jurado murals at the law school? The man himself has just renovated them, you know. Let's take a walk over there.' 'Now?' 'Of course, if you have the time.'"

"Don't you think the onslaught of the cell phone, that insistent call of responsibility in your purse or your pants pocket will soon enough put a stop to such insouciance."

"For sure," said Rufus. "But for the moment—" He glanced at his watch. "Shit, I'm reminded, I gotta go."

Maryanne put her hand on his elbow. "Wait a minute. Look who's here."

A stocky blunt figure, full-length sleeve white blouse and severely shagged brown hair. Amelia Olmsted, who Rufus had known since college and who had been a fellow student in that first graduate contingent of Giles Fort's summer program.

"Don't you want to say hello?" Maryanne drew him with her, leading the way through the crowd.

Amelia was in the midst of some sort of intense, heads together conversation with Evie Swift. Noticing the approach of Maryanne and Rufus pushing toward her seemed more of an annoyance than a pleasure to her.

"Amelia, hi."

"Hello, Mrs. Fort." Much less enthusiastic than Maryanne, wary. But maybe also a little fond, good-old-days fond? It was harder than ever to read her, since her face had lost a lot of its liveliness.

"You all know Rufus," Maryanne said,

Both Amelia and Gini turned and peered at him. "Yes. Yes we do—" they said. Gini added, "Aaron Levine's friend."

Rufus brightened and seemed about to lead with some pleasantry. But the two ladies were deadpanning him, so he stopped, looked down.

"Yes."

Then silence.

Rudeness was one of Evie-or-Gini's specialties, but coming from Amelia it seemed strange. Having known her so long ago, Maryanne felt free to say, "Sorry, I'm a bit of a stranger here by now, so could you give me some idea of what this is all about?"

Amelia looked away, as though she hadn't heard the question.

Gini drew breath, but then stopped. She had in hand a little crockery plate containing the remains of a tamale, the brownish greasy banana leaf wrapping curling out over the edges. She picked at what was left with her fingers, then licked them, picked up the prune which had been inside, ate that, extruded the pit, laid it back on the leaf, licked her fingers again. "Some of us were never as fond of Aaron as Rufus here seems to be," she said finally.

"Is there a reason?"

Gini laughed a chirping little laugh. "Oh no, none at all. Caprice, it's just a caprice on our part."

"No." Amelia entered in as though suddenly awakened from a dream. "There are reasons. The whole Grass Valley thing."

"Aaron told me," said Rufus. "About the ins and outs of his divorce becoming public knowledge."

Amelia seemed willing to let it lie there, but Gini shook her head vigorously, as though the very idea were a gnat she needed to shoo off. Her face scrunched up and she reached out a finger and poked Rufus once in the center of his chest, right on the sternum. "There's a good deal more to it than that!" she said. "The whole disgusting debacle of what was revealed! Hardly surprising if Aaron wouldn't share the real story with you."

"And what's the headline there?"

"Well basically how he forced his wife to share their marriage bed with other men, isn't that right?"

"One man, as far as I know. And at his wife's suggestion. How exactly do we know this, Evie?"

"Well it all came out, didn't it? In the divorce? In the charges that poor abused woman brought."

"Came out how exactly?"

"It was Amelia's parents who saw it in the newspaper up thre and sent along the clippings."

"But California divorce is no fault, isn't it?" Rufus said. "So wouldn't it be unusual for ordinary citizens' complaints about each other to get into the press?"

"But Rufus," and here Evie bent her head to the side, "there were children involved."

"Aaron had no children."

"Foster kids, two of them. Little black fellows. And <u>they</u> may have ended up having been abused one way or another too. It's a certainty, really. They were removed from the situation by Child Protective Services pronto."

Having flung this remark, Gini turned on her sandal heel and stalked away.

When Rufus looked to Amelia for some kind of explanation, she too seemed a little flustered by what had just happened, or at least by being left holding the bag. But then she rallied and in a courteous but tired voice began to ask Maryanne was she planning on doing some work in Manantiales and how long was she staying. When Maryanne said she was leaving in just a few days, Amelia expressed sorrow over it being so soon. Turning to Rufus, she asked after his partner and he had the uncomfortable job of telling her that Javier had been dead a year.

In the way Amelia spoke you could still pick out traces of Park Avenue, the long "a's," the occasional looseness or at least languidness of her lower jaw.

C3

Some called Amelia's life tragic. Rufus thought at least sad. Not to deny anyone anything they deserved, but he didn't like using 'tragic' unless at least some of Aristotle's criteria were being met. With Amelia it would be hard to tell exactly what her fatal flaw had been, though the fall from high position he supposed grand enough to qualify. She had begun an obvious star. A Brearly girl, super-articulate, above all a great deal of fun to be around. Married early to another young star among the anthropology grad students, Bill Olmsted, a direct descendant of the great landscaper. Rufus was present at their wedding, a summer afternoon affair on a long densely green lawn in Greenwich.

Amelia's successes only impelled her on toward even greater successes. She had an enormous aptitude for learning languages, and absorbed facts about the lives of the people she lived with in great gulps, understood implications quickly. Making light of the discomforts of fieldwork, the days and days without a bath, the bugs, squatting in a cornfield in a pelting rain to take a pee, Amelia plunged. In their cohort she had no rival, unless it was Minna Lewis, Rufus's girlfriend of that time. And since Minna was a couple years younger and still an undergraduate, the other students didn't think of the two young women as being competitors. Plus they were good friends. For dissertation research, Amelia and Bill Olmsted went into the Petén, the great rainforest and savannah outback of Guatemala. There some awful things happened, though it was never quite clear in what order or why. A lot of the story depended on Amelia as witness, and in the aftermath of Bill's death she became very close-mouthed. The villages they worked in were early staging areas for the student guerillas from Guatemala City who went operative in the late 1960s. It seemed some of those people became convinced the young couple were C.I.A. They sequestered Bill and when he did not answer questions to their satisfaction they shot him. (But if that was the story, why did they not kill Amelia as well?) Another account laid the blame on a reckless love triangle, a Guatemalan student radical who thought he had won Amelia's affections getting drunk and going after Bill. (In this version, the claim was that Bill was not only shot, he had been hacked to pieces with a machete and was seen by an undertaker in Flores crudely sewn back together with sisal cording into the semblance of a person.) In still another but quite muddled telling, Bill's death had something to do with a sexual relationship with another man, not an Indian but a ladino with a Jeep, a coffee plantation owner's son from half-way across Guatemala. Rufus spoke once at a party with a prep school friend of Bill's who said for sure Bill had been in love with his roommate when they were at Taft, but he wasn't sure the two of them had ever actually "done" anything together.

After Bill's death, Amelia drifted into San Cristóbal, told people she was going to start over, work in one of the highland municipios and meet the conditions to finish a PhD. But she never quite got around to any of this. Property in town was still cheap and for ten thousand dollars she managed to purchase herself a little house, only three rooms and a small garden behind. Her father was a prominent surgeon in Manhattan and there was family money, but beyond the bequest from her grandmother which paid for her house Amelia didn't seem to have much access to funds. Her parents retired and went to live at first in San Diego, then in the hopefully-named community of Paradise north of Sacramento. Those who knew said it was Amelia who systematically began to cut herself off from her mother and father, not the other way around. They would ask her to come home to visit, send her a ticket, but at the last minute she would refuse, find some excuse. They offered to come see her in San Cristóbal and did once, but after that she claimed she was so busy, couldn't spare them the time. Hard up then, Amelia took any work she could find. She transcribed Tzotzil for the Mormon missionaries who were intent on getting the Gospels and the Acts of the Apostles into all the Mayan languages. She did data entry and some editing for gringo anthropologists, later some translating into Spanish. For several years she taught at the San Cristóbal outpost of the state university, until a woman who coveted her job made a stink about Amelia occupying a position which could just as well be filled by a Mexican national. Time went by, several decades, and as her possibilities narrowed Amelia stayed home and fed her cats. She worried the people who still saw her. They thought she was consuming too much of the red wine that comes out of northern Mexico.

"I haven't been in her house for the longest time," Janice said, "but I'm told the beams are unsound, sagging badly under the weight of the roof, and some day the whole thing is just going to collapse in on her."

"And she won't get it fixed?" Rufus asked.

Janice shook her head. "She claims she doesn't have the money."

"What about her parents? <u>They</u> have it."

"Yes, but she refuses to call on them."

Lola was sitting on the floor at Janice's feet, sometimes looking up, then returning to a few urgent strokes of licking herself down the back. Suddenly she crouched a little and sprang, landing on the couch right at Janice's side. She settled in against the old lady's leg, head up until Janice began absently to pet her, then stretched out flat and comfortable.

"What do we do about people who won't take care of themselves?" Rufus said.

"What <u>can</u> you do with a person like that?"

"Then what do we think about them?"

"Think? 'Poor souls,' we think. But wrong-headed, for sure. You can't just give up."

Rufus laughed. "I thought you were the person who always loved quitting."

"Work, yes. Any time. But Amelia is a person who it seems wants to call it quits with life."

"And why can't you reasonably do that?"

"Foo!" Janice put up both hands and pushed them out, as though to get rid of Rufus's question. "You know the answer to that as well as I do."

"I know that disappointment can overwhelm people…"

"Yes, but you have to choose your disappointments."

"Like what? What do you mean?"

"Me, I have my one big disappointment too, but you don't exactly see me giving up, do you?"

"No. But what's yours?"

She laughed at him. "My disappointment? You should know."

"What? The failure of the Revolution to come in your lifetime?"

"It does not seem to be arriving on schedule, does it? And next to that, all other disappointments are minor, aren't they? Irritations. Inconveniences. The body falling apart on us? So what? All just the price we pay, part of the deal."

"Which deal?"

"Life."

"Oh."

The Old One was not always so sanguine. Obviously in a very good mood this morning, buoyed by the outpouring of affection at her birthday party.

"Mitzi asked me the most interesting thing," he said.

"Did she?" Janice poker-faced. Or maybe slightly ironic?

"At the end of the party. She'd had a good deal to drink by then I'm pretty sure—"

"How they can stand all that sweet white wine I'll never know. Gewürztraminer!" Janice said contemptuously. "One little glass and I'm starting a headache."

"Me too. I try to stay away from such stuff. So we were sitting there and she leans over to me and says, 'Now tell me just how it is you do it.' Do what? I had to ask. 'You know, become so friendly, I mean really buddy-buddies like you do with these Indians,' she said."

Janice snorted. "Did you tell her for a start she could stop gypping those nice little ladies who make the dolls for her?"

"I thought of it, but I didn't say it. She was quite serious."

"So what did you say?"

"I pointed out that she might begin by learning a little Maya. 'Really?' she said. 'How would one do that?' Your Shalik was still putzing around outside in the garden and getting his stuff together for his lunch, so I suggested Mitzi might occasionally get him to teach her the Tzotzil words for things."

"And what'd she say to that?"

Rufus laughed. "She said, 'Is that what it's called, their dialect? Tzotzil?' And then she looked out after Shalik for quite a while as though she'd just learned something entirely new and exciting about him. How long has she lived here, Janice?"

"It has been a while. Fifteen years?"

"It was a little bizarre, but somehow touching at the same time. As though Mitzi had finally noticed that the gringo anthropologists and even a few of the Europeans like her— Ulric Köhler maybe—had access to something about life in the municipios she didn't, hadn't even imagined she could ever know before. You know what she said?"

"I couldn't guess."

"She said she had never been entirely convinced that any of 'us' would ever be able to speak whatever it was 'they' spoke." Rufus laughed. "Sort of like <u>their</u> belief concerning the tortillas, right?"

"What's that? Remind me."

"I don't know about these days, but in the communities they used to say you couldn't speak *lengua* if you weren't raised on corn—or more specifically tortillas."

Rufus kept half-expecting for the front doorbell to ring and other guests to troop in, but there had been no sound. Now Beta's comida was ready and they were called to come eat. He offered his arm and Janice took it, leaning heavily, and when they reached the table he held her chair and got her safely slid into it.

At the end of the meal, once the tea was poured, Janice peeled big crumbly chunks of yesterday's dense, cocoa-rich cake out of the Saran-Wrap, as carefully as though she was unwrapping gold. Passing Rufus a little plate, she said, as though their earlier conversation had never been let go, "My brother was another one who suffered from disappointment. I think that's so, though maybe it's sentimental to put it that way."

"What would be the harsher way?"

"To say he was just a crazy, poor guy."

The central fact Rufus knew about Janice's family was that her mother had died early. Janice born 1911, her mother gone by the time the little girl was six or seven. The brother younger. Their father a cutter in the clothing business, a highly skilled one, she said, and until her mother died they lived in pretty nice circumstances—no want--in a flat in Harlem where both children had their own rooms. After his wife's death, Janice's father held them together financially, he still supported them, but he was not the same man he had been and knew it. So except on weekends and for the occasional short summer holiday at a socialist encampment on a little pond beyond Newburgh, the children didn't see him very often. He put them to live out in the boroughs with their aunts—the ones on his wife's side—women who ran large households and had plenty of kids of their own. And that was good, very good, at least for Janice, because the aunts all had big laps and big warm chests to lean against very much like her mother's. Her brother Bobby was not so lucky in the sense that he didn't have a great deal of memory of their mother to hang onto. 'He was not yet four when she passed,' Janice said once.

She herself was no big fan of Freud. But with Rufus she did once entertain the idea that her loving women instead of men was related somehow—she didn't want to pursue it too deep, she said—to losing her own mother and the way she had grieved over that so long ago.

"What did Bobby do?"

"For a job? His work? He was gay, you know."

"No, I didn't."

"I thought I had said. Both children in a family. Is there some reason for that as obvious as your nose and I just haven't seen it?"

"Not that I know, Sweetie," Rufus said.

After a bite of cake and a moment of reflection, she said, "So he was a window dresser, at Macy's finally. He worked his way up. A really good job. In the Thirties there I was in the WPA going through all those dusty folders in the basement of City Hall making peanuts but Bobby was bringing in a real salary. He had his own apartment. I'd go and stay over sometimes, when there was a meeting that ran too late or whatever."

"So what was wrong?"

"Wrong?" She sipped her tea, peered curiously into the cup as though the answer lay there. She huffed once and Rufus thought she might fill up and cry, but she didn't. She did turn to the side, however, face away from him, and gazed out on the afternoon sky show, the shafts of sturdy sun slanting down from breaks in the clouds and spotlighting patches of the south side of town. "He would lose it, Bobby, that's all. He made clothes for fun, men's and women's, costumes for himself and his friends, but daywear also. Suits even, and suits are tricky. He was very good at it, my father had taught him how to cut, maybe thinking he'd follow along into the trade, so why not? It gave him pleasure. But then one time I remember he started carrying a cigar box full of mostly unmatched buttons around with him everywhere he went, back and forth to the store, keeping it right next to him on the table at the automat and all, and going down into the subway at 34th Street one time the darned thing spilled. Rush hour. I was with him, another friend too. And Bobby started to cry like his heart had dropped out of him and there was nothing that would satisfy him but we had to try to help him recover every one of them. Four hundred buttons. In and out around people's feet, 'Excuse me, sir, but I think you're standing on one of my buttons. Excuse me, madam, could you just move your foot?' Nightmare. And then he's counting them and trying to figure out which ones are missing."

"And what happened?"

"In the long run? I was out of the country, in Mexico for my first time, the War had already started in Europe, Dad didn't really know what was going on or at least there was nothing he knew to do and Bobby couldn't take care of himself, that was clear, missed work, wouldn't come out of his apartment or answer the door, so they came and took him and put him in Creedmore out in Queens."

"And?"

"And what? And there he stayed until he could patch together enough lengths of cloth to tie to a radiator and hang himself out the window."

"Oh Janice."

She nodded once emphatically, then set her mouth, turned back to face him.

Rufus was silent. Then he said, "Did he have lovers, friends, happiness sometimes that you know of?"

"Friends, yes. Some good, some more of a problem in themselves, but yes, friends. He was a very attractive person a lot of the time, knew how to make a party out of almost nothing. A piece of cheese and a record-player and a few bottles of beer. Lovers I don't know. It wasn't the time you'd tell your sister about that."

"Even if your sister had girlfriends you knew were her lovers too?"

"Who says that?"

"You did. You said the Party would call you in and question you about the women you were going with."

"Yes, but that was later. After the War. And I would tell them—do you remember?"

"Yes, you would tell them your personal life was none of their business and they could butt out."

Janice had brightened. "Indeed. I was never in the running for Miss Popularity with those guys."

"Do you miss Bobby?"

"Of course I do. To this day. There was a period in there where I was the little mother and he was what? My little baby boy."

"Do you think his big problem was being gay?"

"Well it couldn't have helped, could it? Back then. But there are losses some people just can't get over, and my brother Bobby had them." She breathed heavily. "Poor guy."

☙

"Sometimes," Rufus said, picking up on an old gambit of his and Janice's, "I wonder if our friend Aaron's unorthodox sense of boundaries came from what J. Edgar Hoover did to his father, his family, to him."

"How do you mean?" Janice looked up directly at him.

"You know they say the only way to be read out of the middle class is to commit a murder."

She huffed a little bit, a laugh with irony attached. "But that's not so. Going nuts will get you out, of course, and then of course being called out as a card-carrying Party member. Though I guess theoretically none of us was supposed to <u>be</u> in the bourgeoisie anyway, were we?"

"They were," Rufus said, "the Levines, full-on. Dad a bigtime Renaissance scholar at Columbia, apartment on Riverside Drive, Aaron at Horace Mann and practicing his cello every afternoon. The next Casals. Then that life is pulled out from under them and like thieves in the night they're sneaking back into their own apartment with flashlights to get little pieces of their stuff, and off they drive to Mexico in the family station wagon. Aaron and his sister have to learn Spanish on the quick to continue their schooling, parents eventually driven out of hospitable Mexico due to pressure from the U.S State Department. Pressure. So then off to various socialist paradises—the Soviet Union, Cuba. You know what happened to the old man in the end."

"What?"

"Jerome Levine was still the bigtime Renaissance guy, so he got a job at York in Toronto. And when he died Aaron's mom wanted to bring his body home to the family plot outside Boston. But the State Department wouldn't release the necessary papers."

"Eternal creeps that those guys are. So what happened?"

"Aaron and his sister wanted to put Dad in the back seat and drive him back across the Peace Bridge in Buffalo, but their mother wouldn't hear of it. So they're up there in the ground in Canada, his parents. Aaron too by now."

Janice was silent, looking down.

Rufus said, "Why <u>wouldn't</u> all that turn Aaron into some kind of outlaw?"

"But what about me?" Janice said. "I didn't leave the country under the best of circumstances either."

"You've never quite told me about that. Did the Party want you gone?"

"They told us things were going to get even rougher and for our own sakes they were encouraging the artists and the 'oddballs' as they called us to get out while the getting was good. The problem there was that at the time <u>I</u> wasn't any kind of artist in any shape or form. I think they mainly wanted to get rid of the gay boys and the women who wouldn't wear dresses because we were an embarrassment to them."

"And you had at least had something to come <u>to</u> down here."

"Like what?"

"Lois, remember?"

Janice brightened up, a big smile. "Oh yes, her!"

"In your own sweet way, you've led a kind of outlaw life yourself haven't you, Sweetie?"

"Have I? I suppose I have," she said.

CB

The cane was a fairly new thing for Janice. She claimed there was nothing wrong with her legs—so far, knock wood—that the problem was only she had old Jewish ladies' feet.

"What are those?" Rufus asked.

"You know, feet like mine, like my aunts.'"

She was in the bathroom soaking them in a basin with Epsom salts when he dropped by the house. Beta had been helping her, but after she pat-dried Janice's gnarled ancient toes it was time and Janice encouraged her to go. So Rufus saw Beta to the door, then guided the Old One into the living room barefoot, got the damp towel under her feet and held her by the shoulders as she eased down onto the sofa.

"I'm going out myself, you know, so I can't give you much time."

"It's OK," Rufus said, "I have only one question."

"Really? Slow day, hm? Well ask away," she said. "But before you do I'd appreciate it if you could give me a little more help."

She wanted her tennis shoes and a pair of the white cotton anklet socks she favored and some of the bunion pads she kept in her bedside table. He looked in on the dusty collection of dried-out, contorted flesh-colored pads, but couldn't decide which ones to take her. When he called in to her she called back, "Just bring me the drawer then."

Though not usually a squeamish person, Rufus was glad not to have to sort among the nasty old things himself. In Spanish you might call them 'escabroso.' Janice, however, went rooting cheerfully through the drawer, picking one up to examine it, then another. Luckily, she finally decided none of the older specimens had sufficient stickum left and so had Rufus go into the unopened packet of Dr. Scholl's and cut her some new ones with the nail scissors she also kept in the drawer. He got down on one knee to place them and pull on her socks for her and then her shoes.

"There," she said, wagging her feet back and forth like a little girl. "So. Question?"

"You know about the gossip the ladies spread about Aaron."

"That muck? Of course I do."

"Do you think any of it's true?"

"Does it matter?"

"No, I don't think so. Not to me."

"Me neither," she said. "They drove Aaron out of here and down to Comitán to make themselves feel better about—well, I guess about themselves finally."

"My understanding was that the situation with the third guy—a young man Aaron worked with at the hospital—was entirely happy until jealousy reared its typical head."

"Yes."

"And the two foster kids were an attempt to save them from life on the streets of Oakland."

"That was my understanding too."

"So then there's a second question."

"All right. You said one, but I'll give you two—this time."

"Why would Amelia's parents send 'news' like that all the way down here?'

Janice thought about it for a long moment. Then she shook her head. "I don't know. You're the student of human behavior, aren't you?"

"OK. We both know people love to spread dirt about each other. But this one seems so...I don't know...<u>distant</u>. Fashionable old New Yorkers, physician and wife, people likely of some intelligence reaching out from far away, from 'Paradise' California to fuck with another doctor over what is past and done?"

"I met them once, the time they came here. Amelia brought them around. Lois served hamantashen with the tea I remember."

"Was she messing with them?"

"No, no. It was Purim and she'd found poppy seeds in the market, so she made them. They were delicious too."

"What were they like?"

"Poppy seed, I told you. Or was it prune she made?"

"The parents, Janice."

"Oh. I don't know. Uptight of course. Mexico seemed to scare them, unknown diseases, dirt, rabies. The mother kept wiping her hands on her napkin. But the main thing I got was how concentrated they were on trying to get their darling daughter back in the fold."

"So they'd send the stuff about Aaron just to have a reason to write Amelia yet another letter, stay in touch?"

Janice shrugged. "I'm not a mother, you know— What lengths people will go to—"

The tinkly bell in the corridor was sounding.

"That's either for you or for me," she said.

"OK. I'll go. But you really think that's it, Janice, the reason?"

"Why not?"

"Well, because it's so shitty."

She shrugged again, then said, "But it's a shitty world, isn't it? You knew that."

○3

When Maryanne went by Janice's the morning she was leaving, the Old Girl decided the sala was too chilly and suggested they go out in the sun. She put on an old crushed straw hat and they went and sat side by side on the concrete platform on the town side of the house, Janice with her cane down resting between her legs.

Maryanne said, "Do you happen to remember the Rouses?"

She thought, then shook her head. "Do I?"

"A couple, little husband, somewhat heftier wife. Here around 1970 for about six months, rented that house up on Isabel la Católica behind Na Bolom."

"Well yes, maybe. What about them?"

"One time just to have something to say, I asked the husband—Roger I think his name was—what had brought them to San Cristóbal. And he said, 'Well, I wanted the beach and my wife wanted the mountains, so we came here.'"

Janice gave a little laugh.

"A good while after they pulled up stakes and went away someone, I can't remember who, met up with one or the other of them in some place like San Miguel Allende and it turned out they had divorced. Fairly soon after they left San Cristóbal."

"Really! Who could ever have seen that coming?" Janice's eyes were merry.

"That assortment of people at your birthday party--I was put back to wondering again what it is that draws the foreigners here."

Janice took up her cane and pointed straight out at the city and the mountains on the valley's far side. It was a particularly lovely morning, a few little clouds, sun intense but not burning. "This," she said. "Why would you need any more answer than that?"

"Was it 'this' that lured you and Lois?"

"As I recall, yes. There were hardships to living here in those days, you know, but the beauty of the place, the climate made up for..." She trailed off, then suddenly said, "But you know we were on the run too, some, more than a little, and this seemed a not-half-bad place to hide out."

"On the run from the witch hunt?"

Janice laughed. "Well probably not me in particular, I was never any sort of big fish you know. Maybe on the run from the ruckus we thought Lois's husband might make, and from the atmosphere at home. It was a dark time, you know. A lot of friends turning on friends, a lot of entirely reasonable paranoia."

They sat in silence, absorbing sunlight. Two blocks below was a street used by everyone who drove a taxi. If you were down there it would be very noisy, but though you could see the cars streaming along from Janice's terrace the sound that came up was only the general amenable hum of the city.

"You guys—the anthropologists—you're here on business at least."

"Yes."

"And I needn't tell you out there—" again she used her cane as a pointer, waving it this time in a little wobbly circle, "— actually all around us, are people, how many is it now? a quarter million?"

"By now?" Maryanne said. "The indigenous population? Evan Richards, who follows that sort of thing, says more like half a million or a million."

"A lot then. People who don't always think the way the rest of us do nowadays—"

"And what would you say the difference is, Janice?"

She turned and eyed the other woman. "What? You're the anthropologist, aren't you? You're supposed to know these things."

"Yes, but I want to hear your version of it."

"So is it an older way of seeing things? I guess. But no worse or useless for being old. Much more like the way my own grandparents must have conceived of <u>their</u> world back in Russia. Signs, superstitions. Above all meaning in things, two meanings if you're lucky. Spirits out there in the night. Big God or little gods and goddesses or the saints watching over us, interceding in our affairs sometimes. Knowing whether I'm good to my neighbor or not. Much as I loved taking photographs I always thought the camera was the wrong tool for the job here and that Lois was the lucky one to have paint and what they foolishly call 'abstraction' to try to convey what <u>she</u> could grasp about this place."

Janice stopped. Then said, "And <u>some</u> of the people who wander into San Cristóbal get the attraction of the Indians' way as a different way, and some don't, that's all."

"And some like Mitzi begin to get it only after being here ten, maybe fifteen years?" Maryanne said.

"Hm. You've been talking to Rufus Bright."

Maryanne admitted she had seen him in the street.

"Rufus is too hard on Mitzi. She has a big heart, and it's not entirely her fault that her stuff comes out a little too cute. It sells, you know. And Mitzi has to support herself. If I'd had to live off what I ever made from my photographs, I would have starved to death long since. Here—" Janice was struggling to her feet, "— give me a nice hug and go on. You've got things to do and I've got nothing, or at least nothing special."

CB

Once the snow is finally gone from the North Shore or only little patches remain in the shade of porches and along the base of stone walls, there comes a period when the nights go below freezing but the days warm up some and big winds off the plains or down from Canada blow up sandstorms from what the spreaders have put on the roads. You see children on the way to or from school with tears tracking down through the yellow-brown grit on their cheeks. Maryanne sometimes wondered at herself for liking this time of year—it could last a week or even two—especially since other people hated it so. One reason might be because she was off a farm herself and saw the winds and the swirling dust as not just more of winter's brutality, but as clearing away, making ready.

Though she got hold of Rennie in her hotel room in Mexico City last night, they forgot to say where they would meet at O'Hare. So Maryanne parked and went in and waited with other greeters where travelers came out from customs. Latinos were in a majority in the stream so Maryanne was sure she had chosen the right doors, but then she missed Rennie entirely. The young woman in the pea coat didn't see her mother at first either, then fifty feet along she wheeled and came back pushing her suitcase in front of her. Rennie had cut her hair down to within an inch or an inch-and-a-half of her scalp. It stood up like the bristles on a fine brush and was at first a shock, then pleasing. The girl had a very shapely head, elongated in the back, a fact not even her own mother could have told you. Being less round up top made her appear taller and the body below less bulky. Or maybe in two-and-a-half months of Chiapas Rennie had lost weight.

After a kiss and a big hug the look of surprise must still have lingered on her mother's face for Rennie ran her hand feathering over the top of her head and said, "I'll explain."

In the car while Maryanne was waiting to pay to exit, Rennie announced she'd gotten lice, she wasn't sure where. She had made friends with Shalik, Janice's gardener, and he had invited her to come to a family christening in Chamula and she had ended up spending two nights at his house in a place called Peteh. But she didn't want to blame the lice on that, she said.

"And I didn't want Janice to find out, so I went to Beta and she tried one of those shampoos on me but it seems I had too much hair for it to work. So we went to the market one afternoon and one of the barbers who does the Indian men shaved it all off for me. And that did the trick," Rennie laughed.

"And what did Janice say to that?"

"To what?"

"Your coming in, well—" Maryanne hesitated.

"Bald? I wore scarves for a while."

"And you think Janice didn't notice?"

"Oh no. Janice notices everything, doesn't she? It's her thing really. I don't know what she thought, but when I'd finally grown out enough to take the wraps off, she said I have a shapely cranium and I look good this way."

"Well that's true, you do."

They were within a few blocks of the house when Maryanne said, "I'm sorry to say we're not going to be entirely alone for at least the next few days."

"How's that, Mom?"

"Do you remember Rufus Bright? We all had comida together at Janice's that day you decided to take the casita."

"Yes. Big man, gay. Beard. Janice likes him."

"Yes. Well he's gotten the job of organizing your father's papers for the Newberry and he scheduled himself to fly out and get started before I knew you were coming so—"

"It's cool. Don't apologize. Is he staying at the house?"

"Oh no. He's mostly out in the garage, I put an electric heater out there for him, and he's got a room at a hotel down in Evanston. But I am feeding him, at least lunch. So far."

Enough of a routine had already been established that when Maryanne and Rennie came into the big kitchen at 157 just at noon, Rufus Bright was already in from the garage. "I smell cinnamon and bay leaf and allspice," he said. "Is it *sopa de pan*?"

"That's right," said Maryanne. The foil covering over the large ceramic casserole she had left on the stove was half up. So Rufus knew damn well what she'd been making.

"But isn't that a lot of work?" he asked.

"Not so bad," Maryanne said. The pilot wasn't functioning right so she had to bend to get her match to the burner under the soup. Rufus hovered, irritating her, so she didn't say the next thing she might have, that she'd taken the trouble to make her favorite Chiapas dish as a kind of homecoming celebration for her daughter. Up very early to cook the string beans and the carrots and fry the bread rounds and potatoes and the bananas and then the tomatoes and garlic and get it all cooked together in chicken broth before she had to leave for the airport.

"Remember that hole-in-the-wall in San Cristóbal down across from the old market where *sopa de pan* was the specialty on Sunday?" Rufus asked.

She nodded, then turned and said to Rennie, "You sat at one or the other of two long tables and in the corner just inside the door there was a sink where you could wash your hands and a towel on a nail so you could dry them. The clientele was mostly truckers and other people on the road."

"The meal was ten pesos and if you got a Coke out of the cooler it came to eleven."

"So how much was that back then?" Rennie asked.

Maryanne and Rufus both said, "Twelve pesos to the dollar," then laughed at themselves for overlapping.

Once the soup was simmering, Maryanne gently dropped the fried bread rounds on top and recovered the casserole with the foil. Ten minutes. While Rennie was taking her bag upstairs Maryanne went into the dining room and began setting the table. Rufus stood at the front windows looking out on still Prairie Avenue and the clouded-in day. Maryanne wondered did he remember the old woman who ran that restaurant, Doña Meli, who sat all morning on a low chair in the dirt floor kitchen presiding over a charcoal fire, stirring soup, then tasting, or frying the rice, meanwhile ordering about a whole battalion of talkative, laughing daughter and daughter-in-law helpers. Meli with her head bound up in a cloth and her legs spread wide looking like Maryanne's idea of a gypsy queen.

In that narrow building with no sign out front and in the kitchen no back wall and only a partial roof. Smoke from the charcoal braziers and the fogón trailed off and wafted up out into the blue. Maryanne was about to ask did Rufus remember that too when she thought about her own soup and instead darted back into her own kitchen. You wanted the bread (big croutons, really) to absorb some of the liquid, but not enough to make it soggy.

There must be a reason 'guest' and 'pest' rhyme. Even if they aren't staying with you, visitors are always needing something, putting your things down in the wrong place, trying to help and making mess where there was none. Maryanne had anticipated Rufus as the usual sort of bother. But with him there were other sorts of imposition as well. Whether he meant to or not, he had the habit of trapping her in memories. Not necessarily unpleasant ones, which itself was part of the problem. Because of this past they had shared (and also, a voice inside her insisted, had <u>not</u> shared) he got into her head, took the driver's seat at times she did not want him there at all.

Toward the end of lunch, Rennie asked had either of them heard about Janice's cat Lola. No. Well, it seemed Lola did not come in one evening and then was not to be found the next day either, no matter how often Janice called all over the property for her. Very concerned, she enlisted Beta and Rennie and Hannah Seiden, the woman who helped keep her finances straight, to go out in a posse and look for the animal. When they came back empty-handed, Janice was convinced that someone had nabbed her Lola and would soon be getting in touch to demand money for her return. (Behind her back Hannah pointed out how unlikely this scenario was, but also how touching, since San Cristóbal had a surfeit of cats and Janice was the only person in town who would imagine Lola being worthy of ransom.) Then Janice decided that what was wrong with other people going out to call for the cat was that she really only responded to Janice's own voice. But with her legs as bad as they had become, it would be impossible for her to get around through all the nearby streets where the poor traumatized little thing might be hiding. So what to do? It took the Old One 24 hours to come up with the solution. The next afternoon Janice was lying in wait for the men who delivered bottled water from the truck with the speakers on top, the ones that played a tinkling version of 'Raindrops keep falling on my head' through the city all day every day except Sunday. Could their truck be rented after hours? Yes? And for how much per hour? So that very evening found Janice in the passenger seat of the bottled-water truck trundling slowly through Cerrillo, microphone in hand, calling in her most persuasive voice, 'Come here, Lola, that's a sweet girl, come home now, come on home…'

And did that work? Rufus asked.

In a way, Rennie said. Not immediately, but a day later the daughter of a family down the street showed up at the door with a small black cat in her arms. Janice was overjoyed. At first everyone except Beta was convinced Lola had returned. The cat knew her way around, she got up on the couch and slept next to her relieved mistress, hissed at Buster when he came nosing around her food dish but was otherwise merely dismissive of him.

But then one evening Lola scratched at the doors into the sala and Janice let her in and then 15 minutes later there was more scratching at the doors and when Janice opened up a second time it became immediately obvious that the cat already in the house was an imposter. Even the fake Lola seemed to understand the jig was up, because as soon as she saw the bonafide Lola she jumped down from the couch and made off into the night, not to be seen or heard from again.

The question then became if Beta was not deceived, then why was Janice? Was she so desperate she would accept just any Lola that might show up? Or had she known all along and had just taken on fake Lola because she was so heartbroken over the disappearance of the real one?

"Of course some people jumped right in and decided that Janice is losing it," Rennie said.

"Do you think that's the case, honey?" her mother asked.

Rennie shook her head in a way that made it seem she had temporarily forgotten she no longer had a big mass of hair to move about. Then she thought a bit, aligned her salad fork, and said, "You know about her car, right?"

No, neither Maryanne nor Rufus did.

"She went downtown, I wasn't there, though I usually do try to go with her, and on Guadalupe I don't know what happened but she must have gotten distracted by something and she ran up onto the curb, a fairly high one, and then when she put it in reverse and tried to back off she broke her front axle and knocked the air out of the right front tire.

"When did this happen?"

"A couple of weeks ago."

"Is Janice OK?"

"Yes. She was shaken up a little. The main thing is the police impounded her car and took away her license."

"Ha! Half the cabdrivers in San Cristóbal don't have a license," Rufus said.

"Some of the ladies who watch out for her have told her she has to give up driving anyway."

"Which ones?"

"Greta and that other lady Mitzi."

"And how does she take that? Not well, I'd imagine."

"I was surprised. She seems OK with the idea. I was there, and she just shrugged and said maybe they were right. But she does want the car returned to her, of course, she's got her lawyer onto that already, and she wants to get it repaired."

"But if she's not going to be able to use it?"

"Well, I think the plan is for me to drive her everywhere she wants to go." Rennie laughed a little, head down.

Rufus put his elbows on the table, leaned forward. "So you're going back?"

"Oh yes, sure."

"For how long do you think? Any idea?"

Maryanne wished she could warn Mr. Nosy. Pressing Rennie about her plans only made the girl nervous.

But now she was casual, sunny. "I don't know. I like SanCris. There's a lot that's new for me there, a lot I can learn."

Instead of backing off, Rufus became more intent, a serious eye on Rennie. "Like what? Can you give me an example?"

"Well, for one I get interesting stuff out of Janice."

"Like?"

Rennie thought. "Like the way she looks at photographs. She's very tough on a picture, you know."

"I do," Rufus said. "Tough on others' work, even harder on her own. She doesn't believe any photographer is likely to come up with more than a hundred worthwhile images in a lifetime, you know."

"I've heard her say that. The way she judges portraits also seems harsh to me, but right."

"How's that?"

"If there's any detraction from the subject's dignity, Janice will sniff it out and dismiss the picture. Sometimes I can't even see at first what it is she's objecting to."

"Did she say that to you?" Rufus asked. "About a person's dignity?"

"Not in so many words. But when we look at photographs together, I'm pretty sure that's what's going on."

Rufus nodded. "And of course that's the reason her own portraits are so great."

"Well I think that's the case, don't you?" Rennie said.

The question hung in the air before them for a moment.

ೞ

Maryanne could see some legitimacy in the way Rufus entrapped her in memories, since it was part and parcel of the cataloguing of Giles's papers. She would go out to the garage where Rufus had the desk she had set up for him, a door on two sawhorses. A lamp and the heater on the floor beside him made an oasis of light and warmth in the chilly echoing space where he could detain her. This time when she came to ask him into the house for a cup of tea he had three sets of documents lined up to ask her about, each neatly paper-clipped. Could she put any sort of date on this article? Was that one a final? Could it have been put out under another title? This maybe? he asked, pointing to an item on a complete Giles bibliography he kept out before him on the table. He and Maryanne had agreed—and the Newberry concurred—that intermediary drafts could be tossed, unless Giles happened to have written something interesting in the margins or crossed out a chunk of material so it was unlikely the thought there had ever seen the light of day.

Sometimes it seemed to her way too much poring over entrails, stuff the Great Hoarder himself should have tossed long ago. But now she dutifully inspected the first two sheafs of paper Rufus held up to her, told him what she knew, mentioned what she could infer, another part of her meanwhile becoming anxious over whether the kettle was boiling or whether maybe

Rennie had heard it whistle. How silly of her to think she could pop out to the garage and pop right back.

Finally she had to say it: "Amusing, isn't it? Paper may speak to us, but sometimes it requires a human interlocutor for what it's saying to make much sense."

Rufus sighed, put down his pen. "You know," he said, "now that you bring it up, I have been wanting to apologize for all that prickliness of mine that night at Petra's. I don't know what was wrong with me. Of course talking to the living is just as worthwhile—or as 'clean' or honorable if you want—as mucking about in moldy old files."

"That's alright. I was a little defended myself at that juncture. Maybe spoiling for a squabble? I don't know. But then you did me that tremendous service—"

"I did? What was that?"

"You put me back in touch with Rosie Tu'ul."

"But of course I'd do that, wouldn't I? If I had it to give—"

He took off his glasses and stood, looming. Then he said, "That was an ethic Giles provided, you know. If you had data— crap!--if you had information, you shared it with people in the project if they should need it."

Maryanne often forgot how tall Rufus was.

"You know," he went on, "I wasn't even being quite honest with you that evening. I had a project down in Comitán de Dominguez with Aaron Levine which never went well and once he got sick and then died it really just collapsed, went completely to hell. I wasn't working at archives at all, I was on my way back from Comitán where I'd gone to try to pull together what data there were, interviews with living, breathing people mostly, to see if I could fashion <u>some</u> kind of final report out of it and get the sponsors off our backs. Aaron dead but the reminders of him all around, in the town, at his office-- It was not a good time."

"I can imagine." She was about to ask what they had been studying, but in fact Janice Metz had mentioned it. The sex lives of bisexual men. "Come in soon, will you?"

She had prepared a tray and meant for them to sit in comfort in the living room, but when she got back in the house Rennie—her remarkably transformed daughter Rennie—had already set everything down at the end of the dining table, poured herself a cup and gotten into the cookies. Rufus came in with end-of-the-day chill on his clothing, plunked down, accepted tea, and handed Maryanne a broadside on browning newsprint. In Spanish it announced "40 YEARS OF ANTHROPOLOGY IN CHIAPAS," and then in somewhat smaller type a week of talks, performances, and seminars in honor of Giles, all to take place in the San Cristóbal auditorium over by the church of San Francisco. The date was July, 1983.

"Do you remember all this?" Rufus asked.

"Of course," Maryanne said. "McQuown organized it for him, and the great thing as I recall was that it wasn't only gringo and Mexican academics, but that first generation of indigenous scholars who spoke as well. You weren't there, were you?"

"I was. But I guess we didn't overlap much on that occasion either."

"No." Maryanne passed the broadside on for Rennie to look at.

Rufus said, "They had that posted on the bulletin board at a student café down near the law school, and by '40 Years of Anthropology in Chiapas' someone wrote, "*Y nada resultó.*"

Maryanne laughed a little and Rennie looked up at him.

"'And nothing came of it.'"

"I understand what it means," Rennie said, mildly enough. "And I guess I understand the students' frustration, although on its own the comment isn't quite fair, is it?"

Maryanne glanced at Rufus, expecting he would jump right in. But apparently he too was slowed down by the magnitude of the question. The most obvious result of forty years of anthropology in Chiapas was, of course, a large number of monographs, dictionaries and grammars, a virtual mountain of articles, some documentary film, a huge increase in knowledge about indigenous life available to non-indigenous people should they be interested. It was painful to think that students— many of them future scholars themselves—would so flippantly dismiss the accomplishments of previous generations. But, as Rennie said, 'understandable.' It was <u>change</u>, improvement of conditions the young were impatient for. And in forty years some change had come to the highlands, by now at sixty a good deal more. Not just paved roads and metal laminate roofing in place of thatch, but a birth (actually a rebirth) of indigenous 'consciousness' or pride and economic developments as well. <u>Some</u> Indians were doing well financially, the Zinacantecos supplying massive quantities of flowers they trucked themselves to the markets in Mexico City, people in other communities getting rich at money lending or (it was said) in the drug business. But to these latter changes anthropological research had contributed virtually nothing. Maryanne would admit there the students' cynicism had been warranted.

Not getting anything from her elders, Rennie said, "So what is it, Mom? Mr. Bright? You agree with Evie Swift?"

"Evie has weighed in on the subject?"

"She says in her considered opinion anthropologists are nothing more than tourists with attitude."

Maryanne laughed. "I hope you rushed to our defense, dear."

"I did in fact, Mom. To the best of my ability." Rennie turned to Rufus. "I suppose you're aware my brother and my sisters and I all reacted to the demands of our parents' careers by sticking our fingers in our ears and singing loudly whenever there was any discussion of what they might actually be doing."

"So what did you say...in our defense?"

"I tried not to be harsh. It was at comida at Janice's one day and I didn't want to upset the apple cart. I wanted to say that maybe for poets and some paint artists the self is somehow sufficient as their wellspring, but for others there has to be a there there. Photographers, ethnographers. I ended up praising sitting on your behind in unfamiliar sometimes uncomfortable settings for long periods of time trying to understand people whose language you don't know at first and who the rest of the world frankly doesn't really give a fuck about."

Rennie's cheeks reddened and she turned to Maryanne, "Sorry, Mom."

"I's OK, honey. You're too old for me to police your speech anymore."

"So Chiapas has piqued your interest in anthro a little, is that it?" Rufus asked.

"Well I <u>have</u> begun to read some. Janice has a really nice collection, you know. Seems you people systematically brought her and Lois copies of your articles and your books and wrote them lovely dedications."

"Always pleasure in that," Rufus said. "Like bringing your A papers home from school to your mom."

"Janice does admire accomplishment. And I get the impression Lois did too."

Rufus nodded. "What have you been reading?"

"Well I started with Mom and Dad's book about Manantiales, and now I've been reading some of Minna Lewis."

"That early stuff?"

"Yes. You knew her, right?"

"We became boyfriend and girlfriend when we were first in Chiapas."

"But I thought—"

"That I'm gay? Yes. But I have a somewhat heterosexual past. My students in Florida have trouble with that." Rufus laughed. "They would prefer I was just one thing or the other."

"Minna Lewis was amazing, wasn't she?"

"Yes. She was barely 19, you know, when that first piece was published."

"But her fame was based on what?   That anthology by women anthropologists from the '70s?"

Maryanne said, "Her first fame. And it wasn't just the fact of the book. It was Minna's claim that a feminist anthropology already existed, and the way she showed where the ideas and the potential were already at work." She laughed. "She made a lot of us feel really pleased with ourselves. And glad to be included in that book."

Rennie said, "And then to die so horribly before ever reaching the age of 40. She was my dad's student, right?"

"Yes," Rufus said. "In fact, that was the reason I went to that '40 Years' celebration in SanCris. It was less than a year after Minna's death and I thought someone from our cohort should be present for some reason, represent us for Giles's sake."

Maryanne got up, collected cups. The afternoon had slipped away from them. Outside it was nearly dark. She was planning on taking the tray into the kitchen and not saying anything, but then she thought she could convey it without spin or pique so she put the tray down and said, "Minna may have been Giles's student in the sense that he chose her first and took her to Mexico, but I was really the one she ended up working with her when she was an undergraduate."

Rufus considered. "Hm. Even I didn't know that. No, wait, yes of course, I remember Minna talking about you, but in the period when she and I were coming apart. Funny they don't credit your influence on her."

"You think it's funny?" Maryanne picked up her tray, turned.

"No, of course not. I didn't mean it that way," he said.

"I know you didn't," Maryanne said. "I was just making a little joke."

She hoped Rufus might now pack it in for the day and leave her and Rennie to themselves. Just the fact of his being around had the effect of making her feel she was onstage, needed to perform. But unfortunately when she looked out the back she saw glow in the garage window. His desk lamp had gone on again. A couple of minutes later she happened to glance out again and there was a little wavering illumination—from his flashlight probably—in the rounded smaller window up in the garage attic. Rufus up retrieving more material. What a beetle he was going about his archiving. When he first arrived, she took him up the ladder to make clear which of the squared-off blocks of cardboard file boxes under the plastic were Giles's and which hers. After only four days almost half of the Giles stacks had disappeared, carried down, processed by the busy insect, some to the trash, the rest to square plastic bins bound for the library. Admirable as Rufus's industry might be, she also found it mildly repulsive.

As she stood there, she heard first a fairly distant thump and then some clatter and then, five seconds or so later, a small voice piping 'Help! I'm so sorry! Help!' The faint flickering light in the upstairs garage window was gone.

Maryanne called for Rennie, then she herself ran for it. The girl caught up with her on the way across the back lawn.

What they found was big Rufus on his back on the floor, the file folders he had been carrying and the papers from them out all around. The ladder had come down on him, pushing his glasses up against his face, smashing the lenses, and pinning him down.

They lifted the ladder off and inspected him. A trickle of blood and some little glass shards, but his eyes were open and apparently unharmed. They asked if he thought he'd broken anything and he said he didn't think so, he'd come down pretty firmly on his seat. But when they offered him a hand to get up, Rufus said, "I think I'd like just to lie here a minute and catch my breath. That was fairly scary."

Maryanne went in the house and returned with paper towel, hydrogen peroxide, and a handful of Band-Aids of various sizes. Rufus was still on the floor, Rennie sitting cross-legged beside him. Maryanne carefully unhooked his glasses from his ears, looked in his eyes wondering whether he'd had any concussion, then told him to close his eyes and mopped up blood and little shards of glass.

"My glasses are wrecked, aren't they?"

"I'm afraid so."

"It's OK. I have another pair."

There was only one cut, an inch-and-a-half gash right above his eyebrow. Once she had that mopped at and covered, Rufus said he thought he'd like to try getting up now.

He got to his knees and then with the two women's help stood. Did he feel dizzy? No more than usual, he said, trying a smile. The papers all over the floor concerned him. He wanted to pick them up, but Maryanne said he shouldn't try that, she'd get them. Didn't he want to come in the house and lie down a while or something? No, he said, what he really wanted was just to go back to his hotel now and rest.

And nod off? Maryanne was suspicious, wondering again whether Rufus had been out, wishing she knew what exactly it was you were supposed to see in a person's eyes. But he was insistent, so she and Rennie helped him into his coat and saw him through the house and out to his rental car. He got in very slowly, like an old man, and was slow also getting the car started and pulled away from the curb.

ᥫ᩠

As taxing and sad as his illness was, Rufus's partner Javier was blessed in one way. He had a great and attentive physician to see him through. A friend as well, Dr. Fred had a very open attitude toward medications. If it was there, why not use it? Javier always had a prescription for Vicodin and claimed Dr. Fred said he should take as many as needed to stay out of pain. Javier's notion of "pain" included anxiety and so at times when he took four or five Vicodin beforehand and then drank wine at a party, he would go into a floating, uncommunicative state and then suddenly crash. More than once Rufus found his poor lover in a bathroom weeping uncontrollably and needing to be driven home.

But Javier's belief in the drug remained unshaken, and he was generous, insistent even, about sharing. Rufus didn't like the effects as much as his honey did. If he took Vicodin for tooth ache, he was sure the pain remained and the drug only distracted him from it. If he took even one cap when he was at the university he was likely to glide through the day's accumulating irritations and then some unfortunate student would look at him sideways and Rufus would blow his top.

So he tried always to ration himself. But tonight with no supper in him and the water glass and the little plastic bottle right there on the bedside table, two didn't stop him even for a minute from dwelling on how badly he hurt all over. So he took a third.

And lay there. And lay there, shoes kicked off but still in his clothes. And then when he opened his eyes again, the Hilton Garden Inn had quieted down. The street outside too, no passing vehicles. Time must have gone by, he woozily decided. Then for a while he went back and forth between thinking awake and some sort of dream remembering. It was hard to tell which state was which, and it seemed not to matter either.

Javier first went to Chiapas with him that time Rufus wanted to be present for the festivities in honor of Giles. Javier loved to <u>have</u> traveled, but even before H.I.V. travel itself made him very nervous. He expected things to go wrong, and when they did, he saw the trouble to be proof of Rufus's unreliability. But in Tuxtla once the taxi was hired and they had cleared the airport, Rufus felt he could relax. There was very little reason to doubt Javier would be impressed by what came next.

Before the toll highway was built, the cliché invoked for tourists was that the climb from Tuxtla up into the highlands was a voyage back in time. In two hours the two-lane road covered only 56 miles, but lifted the traveler over 6,000 feet from baking hot country into San Cristóbal's alpine climate, ascending through a long set of switchbacks which crisscrossed the spine of a mountain range. Along the way were strung out the parajes or hamlet communities of the municipio of Zinacantán. At almost every turn enormous vistas fanned out before or down below you, glimpses of the sere plain of the Grijalva River valley, a full view of the deep limestone bowl with a flash of silvery water in the bottom called Navenchauk, which means Thunder Lake in Tzotzil. In 1983 there were still steep dark pyramid-shaped traditional houses with blue smoke drifting out through the thatch and the almost-sheer hillsides were hand-planted in improbably regular rows of corn. Indian women with axes and 70- or 80-pound loads of firewood on their backs and ribbons woven into their braids dropped down suddenly from the pine and oak woods onto the highway, turning away to shield their small children from passing cars and trucks in the folds of their skirts, their bare-boned dogs barking at you.

Up out of hot country the first Zinacantec settlement you came to was La Granadilla, a steep little winding valley covered everywhere with corn brilliant green and already tall and tasseling in July. On a map, the road here took the shape of a true hairpin, so whether going up or coming down you got two takes on the place. The valley came into sight, then you lurched into a full 180-degree turn and lost it, and then suddenly you were coming at it again from the reverse angle. The effect was so disorienting that first-time travelers might not realize that they were seeing the same thing twice.

"Look! It's called La Granadilla," Rufus told Javier, pointing. But he had forgotten. The cab slowed and ground through the turnaround and there was La Granadilla again, and the second vision of it for some reason caused Rufus to burst into tears.

"What is wrong with you?" said Javier.

"This is where my friend Minna worked that first summer we were here."

"I see."

Javier sometimes reacted sourly even to mentions of people Rufus had cared about in the past. But Minna he had met and liked (who could avoid liking Minna at least at first? She engaged new people in such a frank, democratic way). So it didn't seem Javier was being pissy about her, only goofing on Rufus for his sentimentality.

There was more he was about to say, but suddenly heavy rain descended on them. The windows steamed up immediately and the driver had to slow some and wipe repeatedly at the glass in front of him to see out. Then water leaked in along the top of the windshield, a sheet of it coming down in Javier and the cabdriver's laps. The driver started to apologize but Javier only laughed. He turned toward the back seat and said, "Now I see why you put me up front."

"I put you up there so you could see the sights."

"I believe you," Javier said, clearly meaning he didn't.

It had been a shock to everyone who knew Minna Lewis to learn that she had died. She was only 37. The manner of her death was also shocking. Doing fieldwork in the mountains above Cochabamba in Bolivia, she went walking with women from 'her' village on a path above a gorge with a river running down it 80 or 90 feet below. They were on their way to another village eight kilometers away when Minna missed her footing and fell.

Some of her friends in the States wondered if there could have been foul play. But her husband said he never got any sense of anyone in the village disliking Minna, and certainly there was no one with a vendetta against her. He said the entire village grieved for her.

A friend of Minna's who was in Rufus's department at Gainesville told him, "If it had been me I could see it happening for sure. I might well have gone over. But not Minna!"

Meaning, Rufus thought, not about feet, but about how strong the life force was in Minna. Which was true enough.

But he himself had a contrary memory.

That first summer Giles sometimes called on Rufus to do some of the driving for him. Rufus was glad to, it allowed him to see the places other students were living from the wheel of the project Jeep. La Granadilla was almost an hour-and-a-half down the hill from San Cristóbal. Minna knew where in the streets around the old market to find trucks that would let her off there, and she didn't mind climbing up and riding in the open back of the vehicles. But sometimes waiting around for a ride could burn up most of a day. And though she wore a Zinacantán woman's skirt and blouse and ribbons, her complexion and her great fall of curly blond hair marked her as clearly not an Indian. More often than not the ladino drivers would invite her to come sit up in the cab with them and then there would be hands moving over onto her knee or her thigh and squeezing. Young as she was, Minna had the kind of presence that allowed her to remove wandering paws in a firm, no-dice manner while remaining friendly enough with the person giving her a ride not to be made to get out at the side of the road. But Giles worried some for her safety, so often he would ask Rufus to give her a lift down to her field site.

She began to take him in along the paths to the cluster of houses where she was living. She had told the people she was staying with she was married, a convenient lie meant to make her independence as a woman less bizarre to them. Being cast as her husband amused Rufus, since he and Minna had only recently become lovers. Often the afternoon rains had come along and there was no one around to notice the lapse and Rufus had Minna lead the way instead of following dutifully behind him. The paths through the milpa were narrow and slippery and the rain drummed loud on the leaves of the corn high all around them.

In those days Indian women were still going barefoot, but Minna wore thin-soled little leather sandals. And what Rufus noticed then and what came back to him immediately almost twenty years later was how sloppy she was in her walking, feet slapping down in the mud one and then the other carelessly. Minna's looks and her sexiness were the source of a confusion for many people. She was much less in her body and much more up in her head than people thought.

ॐ

It was 10:30 or closer to 11 AM by the time Rufus got to the Forts' the next morning. Instead of parking out front he went around through the alley and got as close to the garage as he could. It had taken another couple of Vicodins to get him there and as he pulled himself up out of the damned little rental Focus he experienced some wooziness and wondered how much he'd be able to accomplish today. Halfway to the garage door he saw Maryanne watching him from the kitchen window. He gave her a little wave and a smile to indicate everything was fine, but she must have seen the way he lurched gingerly along.

Rennie came out from the house and offered to be of any help she could. So while he sat and observed, she gathered up the papers he'd spilled all over the previous evening and put the ladder back upright. Whatever he wanted next from up above she'd be glad to get for him, she said. Then she plunked down and it appeared she was going to wait until he had further instructions for her.

After a few unsettling minutes, she asked whether it wouldn't be a good idea for him to take a couple of days off, wait till he felt better before going on with the job. He explained the Newberry was paying his air ticket and him for a certain number of days' work, so there was no leeway for him to go home to Florida to recuperate and then come back.

"Then why don't you go off the clock and come stay with us until you feel better? We have an extra bedroom, you know."

"I'm not sure your mom would like that," Rufus said. "She's been very nice, but I have the impression she'll be glad to get this business wrapped up as soon as possible and have you to herself for a bit."

"You think? Well let me ask her."

"Oh—"

"No, let me."

"All right."

She went in the house and about ten minutes later returned bearing two mugs of coffee, his with milk in it. He thought she might have talked with Maryanne, but when she took up her post again she didn't mention anything.

"Do you mind if I ask more about Minna Lewis?"

"Go ahead. It's fine."

"What does you guys being 'boyfriend and girlfriend' mean in your case?"

"Are you asking were Minna and I lovers?"

"Well yes."

"We were."

"And how did that work?"

"OK, I suppose."

"No, I mean with you being gay and everything."

"Well, Minna was the first woman I ever had sex with. Though I never admitted that to her. She had a great deal more experience than I did."

"And she was 18?"

"Minna's attitude toward sex was unusual."

"For the time you mean."

"Yes, but even for today she might be considered unique."

"Janice said men just fell at her feet plunk, like pigeons. And a lot of women too, apparently. Is that what you mean by 'unique'?"

"Minna—"

But then the Vicodin made choosing what to say next feel a little like turning handfuls of green beans in a bin at the market and picking out one here, one there.

"Actually, I've seen a couple of pictures of her," Rennie said. "Striking looking."

"Yes," Rufus said, "true. But the critical thing about Minna doesn't appear in photographs. For some reason, which may have had to do with her parents' ambition for her, Minna never seemed to grasp that by dint of being a woman she was supposed to hide how intelligent she was."

"Like my mom then?"

"Oh—not to speak against your mother in any way, but compared to Minna Lewis Maryanne Fort is a <u>very</u> civilized and polite person. Minna would walk into a room full of smarties and right up to the smartest of them and start asking questions or commenting on aspects of their work. It startled people, especially men and especially back in those days when girls weren't necessarily supposed to waltz right in on the sacred precincts of the world of ideas."

"But on her it was attractive?"

"It was. Although there was criticism too. What Janice says may be true, but a lot of women saw Minna as an opportunist, pushy."

"For talking seriously to men?"

"Well they claimed it wasn't only her brains that were on offer. She had lovely breasts too, you know."

"I noticed. From the pictures."

"And just as she didn't see any reason to keep her mind under wraps, she also didn't seem to think there was anything wrong about sharing her body with others."

"Is there? Something wrong I mean."

Rennie was smiling broadly at him.

"Complicated, don't you think? With Minna, her openness sometimes made other women write her off as a slut or something. But it also could lead to a strange absence of jealousy among her boyfriends. The summer we were first lovers, she came as far as Mexico City with another guy, then came on to Chiapas and took up with me. A month or so later the other guy showed up in San Cristóbal and he and I became friends. He unrolled his sleeping bag and slept on the floor of the living room in the house a bunch of us had rented."

"But Minna belonged to you by then?"

"Well, in the sense that she slept with me and not with Calvin, the other guy, yes. But Minna really didn't ever really 'belong' to anybody but herself, at least until she got married. And even then--"

"And she didn't care about gaining a 'reputation' of some sort?"

"Never. She pleased herself, and that was gratifying. Your mom's right, she <u>was</u> the one who helped shape Minna. But your father took a great pride in her too, since he discovered her."

"Do you think <u>they</u> were ever lovers?"

"Minna and your father? Why do you ask that?"

"Just a thing I remember. My dad after the news came about Minna's death, how upset he was. I was only 12 or 13, but I was the last one still at home so I was pretty aware of my parents' moods. He was taking me somewhere, to a dance class maybe? and in the car at a stoplight tears began rolling down his cheeks. So entirely unlike him it frightened me. That's all."

"Well—" Rufus hesitated, then decided to go ahead. "That first summer, I was out in Chamula and with Minna being way down in La Granadilla we got to see each other only for a day or so a week when we'd come into town. She'd been in your father's freshman seminar on the ancient Maya, so they shared an interest I was consciously not involved with. In fact, at the time I found the whole obsession with life before the Conquest ill-placed if not exactly creepy. Here were all these living breathing Mayas, but the tourists and the <u>National Geographic</u> and everybody only paid attention to their ancestors. So I kept my nose out of the past on purpose. A highly righteous position, and the only excuse I have for it now is that I was young.

"In August, late, when we were finishing up and about to start back to the States, Giles gets word of a cave up in the northern part of Chiapas where he was told there was old painting on some of the walls. So he takes the Jeep and goes, and doesn't invite anyone along except Minna. I was a little put out with her—it was a weekend we could have had together—and when they came back she didn't have a whole lot to say about their adventure. It was a long drive, the roads were bad, it took them a day to find someone who could lead them to where the cave was, then more time getting the man who owned the property to let them go see it. Did it turn out there was original painting in the cave? It seems there was, several glyphs and a number of heads and torsos of what were probably gods, the remaining pigment threatened by mold. But the owner wouldn't let them take photographs in 'his' cave, so the best they could do was make some pencil sketches.

"When I asked her where she and Giles had stayed, Minna was vague. Oh, they had camped out, had to cook for themselves too, since the local people were suspicious and wouldn't feed them even though they offered good money. I would say the way she glided over the sleeping arrangements made me suspicious, but with Minna suspicion—like jealousy—hardly seemed worth the time and effort."

Ë

Rufus's last afternoon in Wilmette the van from the Newberry arrived at 3 PM right on schedule, and two pleasant, thickset young men loaded up the boxes full of Giles's papers and in about ten minutes were done. Rufus remained at his temporary desk, but Maryanne went out and waved the van off down the alley. When she came back in, she pretend-dusted her hands against one another, sighed, and said, "Well, that's that." But her eye was on the cardboard barrels of the stuff that had been discarded, six of them standing full against the wall.

"You want me to figure out what to do with all that?" he said.

"Don't bother. I can feed it to my regular trash people little by little." She laughed sharply. "You don't make much, you know, when you're just a little old lady living alone."

"Don't make much trash?"

"That's right."

Far from 'little old lady' as she was, Rufus couldn't help wondering if Maryanne wasn't just fishing for a little sympathy.

Supper that evening was in celebration of his mission being over and done, although the food was not fancy, split-pea soup with ham, salad, a heavy-crusted loaf of *pain du campagne* from the French bakery, wine, ice cream. In five days staying at Prairie Avenue, Rufus had noticed a marked decline in the trouble Maryanne took over meals. She knew all the shortcuts of a working mother, skillet lasagnas, Costco chickens. The pea soup she had made in her crock pot on the weekend. He didn't mind at all. The simpler food and occupying the room off the kitchen that had once belonged to the son they called 'Junior' gave him the feeling of being nearly family to the Forts.

Rennie had begun to clear the table when the phone call came. She listened a while, nodding and agreeing but frowning, before Maryanne asked who it was. Rennie put her hand over the receiver and said, "It's Hannah Seiden, calling from Janice's house. Janice has taken another fall."

Maryanne got up quickly and stood by Rennie, waiting for her to hand over the phone.

What Rufus understood when Maryanne and Rennie returned to the table was that Janice had probably broken her other hip. That was the opinion of the SanCris doctors, although she was in such pain they hadn't been able to move her to where they could get an X-ray. She was refusing to consider having her hip fixed in either San Cristóbal or Tuxtla and adamant about being air-ambulanced to Houston to be dealt with by the same doctors who had treated Lois. Hannah said there was no use in trying to explain that Lois's heart doctors would definitely pass Janice on to other colleagues. She had tried.

"Are they going to do it, get her to Houston?"

"It seems so," Maryanne said. "The reason Hannah called is that they're looking for someone to accompany her."

Rufus said, "I wish I were in better shape. I'd go. Although, you know, I'm probably not the best choice."

"Why is that?"

"If there were routines that had to be imposed on her, bed rest or whatever, I'd fail. My batting average with getting the Old One to do <u>anything</u> is a nice round zero."

Maryanne considered. "I could go."

Rennie said, "Or I could. But what would that mean? I'd have to get back to SanCris right away in order to fly to Texas with her?"

"Or you could meet her in Houston. I don't know."

They decided to call Hannah back. Rufus had the number in his cell phone directory so he lumbered to his feet and went to the telephone and dialed. Beta answered and then put Hannah on. Since Hannah knew Janice's financial situation, Rufus's first question was what the air ambulance would cost. Fourteen thousand dollars U.S., Hannah said. She had already checked. And could Janice afford that? Not really. She had the money, but it would nearly wipe out her savings and she would be left without a cushion of any sort.

"But she's intent on doing it?"

"Absolutely intent," Hannah said. "Unshakable as always."

So Rufus went ahead and apologized for his own present lameness, and then offered the services of either Maryanne or Rennie.

"Oh that is very sweet," Hannah said. "But Evie Swift has just been here and she has agreed to take Janice to the States. She has gone home right now to get her things together."

In the calm that followed, the three of them sat a while at the table. Rufus said, "Poor Janice. It's not easy in the end if your basic stance in life is to be obstreperous."

"Indeed," said Maryanne. And then she recounted the story of her goodbye visit to Petra and Sandro the afternoon Janice had come and taken back the two paintings by Lois and the Lois transglow she had sold them.

Rufus had not heard this story, and it puzzled him.

"But you know what that's all about, don't you?" Rennie said.

"I have no idea."

"It's Evie. She's been working on Janice for a while now and has her convinced that Lois's work is due for a sudden huge resurgence—"

"Resurgence? Wouldn't it have to have been known before to have a resurgence?"

"Well, OK then, maybe the pitch is that Lois is about to be 'discovered' and her paintings will soon be worth much more than anyone knows."

"And Janice believes that?" Rufus said.

"Of course she does. It's what she longs for for her sweetie pie. Evie's also worked out a deal so Na Bolom will purchase everything of Lois's and restore it, and they will give Janice a big show and pay her for the inventory of her photographs she's printed herself and all her negatives as well."

"But she's already agreed to turn her own work over to the Newberry."

"Except the Library never offered to pay her anything, and Evie's deal involves cash."

"But the Na Bolom people don't <u>have</u> cash, do they?"

"Well, there's debate about that. Evie says they're due for a big infusion from some place—investors or something—and meanwhile Janice is to begin receiving installments, a monthly check from them."

How foolish, Rufus thought. He wanted to be angry at Janice (he after all had brokered the deal with the Newberry), but the idea of her lying probably in her own single bed waiting for a van (the station wagon of friends? what? an ambulance if she was lucky), people to come jostle her onto a board and cause her even more pain, get her out of the house and to the SanCris airfield and aboard the little plane— All that made it impossible to grudge her for her decision. What was the Newberry to her? How did she weigh the importance of a relatively 'permanent' prestige home for her life's work against the promise of a regular check plus the fame for Lois which had not come to her while she was still here?

ॐ

Rennie and her mother had gotten the rental people to take the Focus back early. The company was willing to receive the car at their Evanston office instead of O'Hare, so Rennie drove it down and Maryanne followed and brought her home. Which meant there wasn't anything for Rufus to get done the morning of his departure but pack. He called to Maryanne to ask should he make up the bed, but she said no, just bundle up the sheets and his towel and she would put them in the machine.

He trundled his bag out into the kitchen and handed her the things to be washed. "I'm ready," he said, whenever you want to go."

"There's been a change," she said. "I'm not going to take you. I've called for a town car, they'll get you to O'Hare."

"Oh, OK."

"Why don't you just wait out in the front room? They'll honk and you should be ready."

"All right."

Why the sudden sourness? Had she suffered a bad night's sleep?

All of the living-room chairs and couches were low-slung. Rufus didn't want to risk getting into one and having trouble getting out, so he stood. The day was promising, morning sun had crossed the front porch of the house, but not yet begun to warm the room. Rennie came jouncing down from upstairs with her coat on.

"I'm going," she said, coming toward him to give him a hug, "so I'll say goodbye now. When are you coming to SanCris again?"

"Probably not till summer."

"I should be there, so I'll see you."

"Good. I remembered something last night after we went to bed that you might find useful. Your father's definition of what anthropology is all about."

"What's that?"

"On the last day of his introductory course, he would tell the students this story about a very rich woman who happened to be a descendant of General George Armstrong Custer. So she bought land overlooking where the Battle of the Little Bighorn took place and built a grand house there and commissioned an Italian artist to paint a mural of 'Custer's Last Stand' for the main hallway. Then she was in Europe and didn't come back until the house was finished and the mural ready to be unveiled. She threw this huge party and with the artist standing by she pulled the curtain and there were a large number of buffalo with halos and huge numbers of Native Americans on the ground having sexual intercourse in a variety of positions. Outraged, the lady turns to the artist for an explanation. He'd read up, he says, and his mural depicts General Custer's last words, which were, 'Holy cow! Look at all those fuckin' Indians!'

"'And that,' your father would say, 'is pretty much what anthropology is all about.'"

Rennie laughed. But her mother, who had just come into the room, said, "I sincerely doubt Giles would have said 'fucking' in front of three hundred students."

"Well maybe it was 'effing' then."

A light tapping on a car horn, a dark sedan double-parked on the street, Rufus's ride. Rennie embraced him again, touching her cheek to his, and was off toward the back of the house. Her mother went and opened the door for Rufus, then followed him out onto the porch.

"Well," he said, hoping the change of plan about taking him to O'Hare didn't mean much, "I have a great deal to thank you and Rennie for."

She said, "I think you should know I do not at all appreciate your telling my daughter tales on her father."

"The 'fucking Indians'? I meant no harm."

"No. About Giles having an affair with Minna Lewis."

"I didn't say that. I told Rennie I never got much of an account of the time they went away together to have a look in some caves, so I was left to wonder."

She shrugged, turned her head, definitely a brush-off. "Whatever it is, I don't want to hear it."

The driver released the trunk catch so Rufus could put his bag in. But then, having a look, he got out to help. Once Rufus was settled in the back seat, he pushed the button to roll down the window to see was there anything he could say to salvage the situation.

But Maryanne leaned down and spoke first. "You know, don't you, that if you hadn't been going today I would have thrown you out of my house? I should never have allowed you access to my husband's papers at all."

"Do you think Giles didn't have affairs then?"

"Driver?" she said. "You'd better go. This man's flight is at noon."

Maryanne's scolding him for his indiscretion was one thing, but the desire to cast him out something entirely more painful.

At least for the moment she seemed to have lost sight of the fact that he too was willing to be a keeper of the Giles Fort legacy, was not in any way a detractor. Or had she somehow managed to suss out there <u>was</u> an old deep resentment which even at this late date might make Rufus want to bring Giles down a peg or two? Not concerning Minna but because of Giles's cocksure pronouncements, his my-way-or-the-highway, an attitude that became more pronounced the longer you worked under him. Giles's fear of letting you go, you growing up and becoming a rival? Withdrawing and going to study with entirely reasonable Murdo McCloud now seemed the best decision Rufus had ever made.

A little strange that Rennie should turn around so quick and tell her mother his guess about Minna and Giles and their lost weekend. He liked Rennie and was of the general opinion that younger people today (his own students for example) were less uptight about someone sleeping with someone else, married or not. What was it after all? A coupling, an exploration. Fun. With Minna often there was also an element of her verifying herself. And if you wanted to call that 'conquest', you had to note also that Minna never lorded it over anyone just because she had fucked them.

◌

It was the first of August before Rufus could get free of Gainesville and off to Chiapas. As usual, the morning after

he arrived in SanCris, he dutifully presented himself at Janice's
door. He rang the bell and waited long enough so he began
to think no one had heard it, but then Beta came. There was
something old-fashioned in the way the young woman greeted
you when you returned after a while away, a courtly but entirely
honest delight.

She led him along into the living room where every possible
surface had been cleared off and 8 x 10 photographs laid out,
Janice and Rennie Fort bent over them hardly looked up when
he came in. It was a surprise to see Janice stumping from image
to image with the aid of a metal walker. The story put about
had been that everything had gone well in Houston and she was
more or less back to normal.

Finally, Janice sighed and braced herself, came upright
and gave him a big smile. "Come see what you think," she said.
"We'll need your opinion." They were trying to decide which
photographs should go in Janice's show at Na Bolom. There was
only wall space for about 40. The definites were lined up on
the low bookcases under the windows, guarded or at least lazily
watched over by Buster, who lay stretched out up on his usual
high perch. Still-in-contention pictures filled the dining table
and the bookshelves on that side of the room, the rejects were
already laid aside in a flat photo paper box.

Rufus almost at once noticed the top photo in the rejects
was a favorite of his, a beautiful, bemused adolescent girl with a
large full sack on her head. The contents must have been grain
or beans, since the sack drooped heavily on both sides, putting
the girl's face in semi-shadow, which had the effect of lighting

up her eyes and emphasizing her bemusement. Rufus picked the image up and took it to the Old One.

"Sweetie, what's wrong with this one""

Janice squinted, scowled at it. "I don't know. You don't think there's something cutesy about it?"

"I don't, no."

Rennie had come over. She said, "It's sure clear that girl likes having her picture taken, isn't it?"

Janice took the photograph, tilted it down to get more of the window light on it. For a long moment she seemed a little lost. Not there. Then she handed the girl with the bag to Rennie. "All right," she said, "if you people think—" And she shrugged a little and worried open a space for it on the accepted side.

Same old Janice. Despite the new physical limitations. Rufus was glad to see it. One time he had copied out a passage from a Lyndon Johnson biography about the number of people—50, 60 sometimes—that Johnson might consult before making a decision, brought it to Janice and asked her who it sounded like. She couldn't see it. "Like you, Janice!" "Me? Like Lyndon Johnson? I don't think so, pal. Not in a million years," she said. "I don't have his ears."

If it weren't for her ability to see in the world things the rest of us miss and, as they would say in Rufus's family, her being able to charm the birds down out of the trees, he would have put nay-saying and rendering judgment first and second as Janice's defining characteristics. The woman who loved nothing better than quitting a job and who questioned everything you said, only grudgingly giving in when she ran out of things to pick at, including imagined faults in her own pictures.

Lois had been the same way, though somewhat more gentle about it. Their style was solidly New York and Jewish and obviously decidedly old lefty, but as Janice always pointed out even among the comrades she was a thorn in everybody's side. As Communists they fashioned themselves the Friends of the Negro, so when they occasionally managed to recruit one the Party bosses would fast track him to rise through the ranks. And then that pesky Janice would spoil everything by putting questions about the guy's credentials.

There were delicate souls who couldn't withstand the way the ladies hectored you and hated it even more when they switched gears and went hurt Jewish mother on you. "You're not coming back until <u>when</u>? Summer? Summer sounds like an awfully long time off to a lady nearly ninety, you know."

Rufus was due back for comida, but he had errands to run, so Rennie accompanied him out down the corridor, Janice stumping along behind them on the walker. Shalik the gardener had shed his wool chamarra and in his shirtsleeves and a pair of baggy old Nike running shorts was whacking somewhat tentatively at the wall between Janice's and the casita with a pickaxe. He hadn't gotten very far. The whitewashed facing layer had come off in several big spots, revealing the brown adobes underneath.

Before Rufus could ask, Janice said, "It's served its usefulness, hasn't it? And think how nice it will be for Rennie to have the whole garden to enjoy." Then, more confidentially, she said, "Besides, she's over here all the time anyway."

As it was, for the moment Rennie still had to go out on the street to get to her own place. At her door, she asked Rufus, "Well, what do you think?"

"About Janice? I was surprised at how limited her mobility is."

"Well you know she got all antsy to come home right after her operation and basically was only in rehab for a day or two."

"That's too bad, isn't it?"

"Yes, but apparently there was no arguing with her. Great as Methodist Hospital is in her estimation, Houston is sickness and strangers ordering her around—"

"And SanCris is home and where she can order around others."

"Exactly." Though there was no one anywhere near them, Rennie lowered her voice. "Did she seem vague to you?"

"I didn't think so. Why?"

"The Mafia girls—Greta and Mitzi—they brought in this visiting German psychologist friend of theirs to examine her—"

"And Janice put up with that?"

"She did. I was surprised too. After he interviewed her the psychologist's considered opinion was that she is severely depressed so he prescribed her some pills."

"And she takes them?"

"She says she does."

"And have they cheered her up?"

"She says if they've come up with a pill for loneliness she hasn't heard about it yet. She has some for pain too. Those she's more willing to go with, though she claims they make her fuzzy or woozy sometimes."

"And you, how are you doing, Rennie?"

"Fine. Better than that."

"That seems about right to me."

She had kept her hair very short and was now considerably slimmer and happier than the young lady he'd met at comida in February.

"I have you to thank for one thing."

"What's that?"

"It turns out to be a big help to me to have my father knocked off his pedestal and made back into an ordinary human being."

"I'm not sure I meant to do that. Your father was quite an excellent ethnographer, you know."

"Yes, sure. But I meant the other thing. Him not being some kind of impossible saint, the dad who never strayed."

"Is that what you were brought up to believe?"

"Sort of. Yes, I'd say it was."

Coming in on Rennie and the Old One bent together over the photographs Rufus had passed through a moment of bitter jealousy. Rennie occupying a place in Janice's life which not so long ago had been his. But the feeling passed, and quickly. He after all could only come and go, and at least for the moment Rennie was a constant for Janice.

Like the motion in him when he found out Janice was giving Na Bolom her work and Lois's. The old story about that place was that even when there was a librarian, the books at Na Bolom all proved strangely capable of developing little feet and walking out the front door. The same with Frans Blom's Maya artifacts. Too tempting for visitors on the tour of the house not to pocket one or two now and then.

So in the end something similar would happen with Janice's photographs. But what did that matter to her. The Newberry? Feh! as she would say.

"I see you've decided not to let your hair grow out," Rufus said.

Rennie reached up and ran her palm forward along the top of her head. "You like it?"

"I do. You didn't have a recurrence of bugs, did you?"

"Oh no," she laughed. "What you see here is choice, not necessity."

℘

By the time Rufus came back for comida, Janice seemed to have considerably less energy. She ate, chewing carefully, but bent over much more than before, her head not far above her plate. At the moments when the usual rituals required it, she roused, starting the little browned potatoes around, a little shaky as she lifted the wooden bowl to the center of the table so her guests could get at the salad.

Only Rufus and Rennie and Evie Swift, who as usual blew in at the last possible minute. Toward the end of the meal Evie adjusted herself in her chair and launched into an account of her accompanying Janice to Houston. How <u>she</u> managed to get them to let her set up a cot and sleep in Janice's room, as Janice had done the times Lois was taken to Methodist. How when they found out it was some young whippersnapper who was set to operate on Janice's hip, <u>she</u> Evie insisted on the head of service do the job instead, and got her way.

Janice was the only one still eating. As she chewed she watched Evie, but in a kind of startled or wondering way, as though all of this was hardly about her. Rufus wondered if she hadn't turned off her hearing aids.

"So that was Thursday night they operated," Evie said. "Friday they moved her out of Intensive Care and back to her room. Then the next day they came and wheeled her over to the Rehab Unit, where there was no room for me to stay. They told me to book a motel or something, but I said the hell with that and spent the night on a couch in Reception. Monday they came in and made her get up and then tried to get her to walk. Quite obviously it was all too painful for Janice, but they weren't taking no for an answer. So once they left her alone, Janice said to me, 'Get me out of here. I want to go home.' I got hold of her doctor and he said oh no, he couldn't release her until rehab certified her for walking on her own. So I just went and booked the air ambulance and then I went back to the doctor and said,

'Sorry, pal, my friend is checking herself out and we're leaving tomorrow, Tuesday. Isn't that right, Janice?'

Janice stuck up one finger as though making an objection. "I don't think so. Why would you want to go on a Tuesday?"

Trying not to laugh, Rufus looked across and could tell from the play at the corners of her mouth that Rennie was also suppressing amusement. Evie sighed and looked off a moment. She didn't seem actually disconcerted, but her tale ended there.

Rufus couldn't fault her for having gotten Janice out of Houston. As he had imagined, had he been along with the Old One he probably wouldn't have been able to withstand her either. But he did know what Evie apparently didn't, that rehabilitation is serious business. If you can't get to the place they want you to, then you're not going to have an independent life anymore.

⅓

The opening of Janice's photography show at Na Bolom turned out to be an occasion people remembered and talked about for a long while. Because of her walking problems, Janice was brought by Hannah Seidin in the back of Hannah's Suburban wagon and lifted down into a borrowed wheelchair. Rufus pushed forward to help, but Rennie Fort had the whole thing thought out and three young men already chosen to assist her. It was nearly nightfall, lamps had been lit, but the western sky was still lurid red with the last of the sunset. A whole gaggle of guests were just reaching the house and when the three young men set the Old One gently onto the pavement everyone applauded.

Janice was all decked out in a densely embroidered huipil, someone had combed up her hair and maybe even put a little make-up on her, and she was wearing the Spratling silver necklace she had bought herself as an extravagance on her first trip to Mexico in 1940. Watching from the sidelines, Rufus allowed himself to imagine for a moment that Janice might as well be the renowned Lady Xok of the ancients returning in her litter to Yaxchilán and he and the others her loyal courtiers. Wheeled up the incline of the little entry hallway by Rennie, Janice confronted a six-foot-high poster announcing the show. Above the lettering a greatly enlarged black and white photograph taken sometime in the mid-50s when Janice and Lois first came to Chiapas. Lois below wearing a headscarf and in sharp profile looking left, and Janice up above in the window of a bus, squinting down into her first Rolleiflex and shielding the viewfinder against glare. On her left hand what looked like a wedding ring. Janice contemplated the photograph a long time, then shook her head and murmured to Rennie, "I hardly recognize them."

Yet there was nothing else vague about her that evening. Had she gone off the wretched pills prescribed by the German? She seemed to recognize everyone presented to her, whether she really knew them or not. Evie Swift swooped about, shouldered Rennie off the wheelchair handles in order to tour Janice through the two-and-a-half rooms where the selection of her work was displayed. Then Evie stood by the big poster receiving visitors and making sure they understood the enormous effort she had put into the mounting of Janice's show.

Since he had to be up in the morning, Rufus left early. Janice had conned him into taking Rennie to Zinacantán for the big day of the fiesta of San Lorenzo, the municipio's patron saint. She insisted they needed to get there by seven a.m., because that was when the "doings" as she called them got started, the processions and the dancing.

Once on the road out to the municipio, Rufus asked, "Do you know a gentleman named Miguel Briceño? Janice introduced him to me last night as though he and I must be old friends. Round little fellow, blue suit, big mustache, jolly?"

"That's Janice's new lawyer from Tuxtla," Rennie said.

"Certainly a flirtatious fellow."

"Is he? He brought a wife and a couple of girl children to the house one Sunday."

"Well, maybe just the opportunistic type. Does he come around a lot?"

"Some. Janice is remaking her will, you know."

"I thought the disposition of their things was all settled years ago, Lois's relative gets something and one of Janice's cousins inherits the house--"

Rennie shook her head. "The cousin is long gone, I believe, though I don't know why." She laughed. "It's for sure there's a growing number of people who think they deserve the house."

"For what reason, do you know?"

"Services rendered. Undying loyalty. Something. Again, I don't really know."

In Zinacantán center, Rufus parked and they walked up to the main street and the market beside the church. Janice was right of course, no tourists yet, but things were humming, large numbers of Zinacantecs up and about, skyrockets kicking out overhead in the pale blue, the dangerous hand-held lead explosion-makers going BOOM! BOOM!, the smell of incense and gunpowder in the air. Flute and drum music, the tinkling of a harp and the sweet sawing of a violin somewhere out of sight. Groups of male officials in black with long red scarves wound around their heads praying and bowing before the pine-bough draped entrance to the church.

Rufus felt fairly at ease. In the old days when he came to fiestas here it was as a visitor from Chamula, the neighboring town. But a lot of the etiquette was the same. In the church he knew to bow to the saints and when to cross himself, when to make a cross of his thumb and forefinger and kiss it. His Tzotzil, never great, had gone to hell, but he could still greet people and perhaps amuse them with a polite phrase or two. He made funny mistakes, calling men younger than he was "uncle," or "older brother," because that was how he had addressed their fathers or grandfathers 35 or more years ago.

<u>What have you have become?</u> he asked himself. <u>A tourist with attitude</u>, self replied.

If you took gringo friends along, the exoticness of these occasions, the drinking and the crowds shoving and the noise would sometimes cause them to freeze up, or at least tire of the whole thing quickly. But Rennie Fort had been to some fiestas by now and knew what to expect. She accepted a shot glass of rum when the drink pourer for a group of officials handed it to her, made silent salutes with the glass, and then tossed the liquor off in one gulp like a pro.

She and Rufus sat on a long shaded cement bench outside the church courtyard to rest and reconnoiter.

"You weren't there at the end last night, were you?"

"No. What did I miss?"

"I had Janice wheeled out into the hall and we were waiting for the car to come around and get us. Evie Swift didn't see us, she was schmoozing some of the guests. One of them was going on about what a great and heartening tale the love of Lois and Janice makes, and Evie said yes, unless you knew what <u>really</u> went on between those two girls. And what was that? the others wanted to know. Evie said, 'Well, the anthropologist Maryanne Fort remembers waiting in the car with Janice outside Na Bolom, right here in fact, and Lois had said she'd only be a minute and when she didn't come, Janice honked for her, and then when she still didn't come Janice just <u>sat</u> on the horn for about three minutes making one hell of a racket!'

"And the others were all laughing and surprised and Evie still didn't see us, so she went on about how Lois's diaries are full of bitterness and anger toward Janice. Truly mean stuff she has to say about her."

"And Janice?"

"For someone who claims to be hard of hearing, it looked like she was taking in every word."

"Did she say anything?"

"No. Evie finally turned and noticed us and <u>she</u> of course had the face of a little girl caught with her hand in her mother's box of chocolates."

A stream of men, thirty or forty of them, some in black chamarras and some in white, most in broad-brimmed ribboned hats and carrying silver-headed canes, came down from the churchyard and began finding themselves seats along the wall down from Rufus and Rennie. They were the civil officials of Chamula come to Zinacantán to pay their respects to their neighbors' patron saint. With them were their wives, who waited while the men engaged in some good-natured jostling and shifting about to get themselves in the order they thought they should be seated in, then put their shawls down and sat on them. Bottles appeared from bags and were lined up on the ground, large Coca Colas and clear Chamula aguardiente, and the pouring of drinks one by one and everyone's salutes to everyone else began.

Had they come down along the slippery paths over the mountain in the moonlight as they did in Rufus's day? More likely by now they'd rent a truck and come around by the roads standing up in the back. Preparations for this visit began the afternoon before with the officials washing their silver-headed canes in rum and salt and then drinking the liquid. The year he came by foot Rufus was only 22, but although perfectly happy, by this hour of the morning he was considerably the worse for wear after almost eighteen hours of boozing and almost no sleep.

It was then, sitting on this same bench in the shade and at about the same hour, that he noticed a girl go stalking by wearing an Indian blouse and ribbons and skirt but in sandals and with a great curly mass of blond hair. He called to her, "Minna!" and she did not hear so he called again, "Minna Lewis!" and she turned, saw him and came over. She was at the fiesta with the family she lived with in La Granadilla, and she too had not slept much and had been drinking some, though decorously, in the style of women. Neither of them had washed for a number of days, but when Rufus sniffed at Minna's hair and then at her shoulder, all he could pick up was wood smoke and copal and a very light pleasing sweat saltiness.

Should he try to convey to Rennie what that meeting so long ago had meant? The moment he had been most in love with Minna.

But Rennie had other concerns. "Do you think there would be a way somehow to <u>shield</u> Janice from some of these people? She's so great, but she doesn't seem to be able to distinguish anymore between the ones who wish her well and the ones who really don't."

"Well, you're the one who's closest in now, aren't you?"

"Oh—"

"No, I mean you're <u>there</u> and maybe you could watch out for her a little?"

"I suppose—" Rennie considered. "I owe her, you know."

"How's that?"

"She's got me started painting again. I don't know exactly how she did that, but she did."

"Do you show her what you're doing?"

"Sometimes, not always. She doesn't criticize me, she's really only encouraging." Rennie laughed. "She thinks Lois's spirit has come into me. What do you think of that?"

"Well-- Let's argue that one by negatives: what would the reasons be for that <u>not</u> being true?"

"For one person's spirit to migrate into another person's body?"

"Yes. And be careful," Rufus said, looking up and down the street, "remember at the moment you're surrounded by five thousand or more people almost all of whom believe souls do escape the body and wander, in multiple parts or as wholes."

They stayed until the bells in the church rang noon and men took off their hats and a whole barrage of skyrockets shot up and exploded in little puffs of white smoke. On the way back to the car, Rennie said, "There <u>is</u> one real problem I have to face, you know."

"What's that?"

"Janice wants me to finish Lois's last big painting, the one she was working on when she died."

"And why wouldn't you want to do that?"

Rennie shrugged. "Because I might royally fuck it up?"

"And more important somehow disappoint the Old One?"

"Well yes, I suppose that's the real reason I don't want to touch it."

Back at Janice's, Rennie wanted Rufus to see how far Lois had come on the painting and the sketches she'd done for it. The piece leaned against the wall behind some smaller pictures in Lois's room. It was four or five feet by eight or so. What Rennie pulled out and turned toward the light was a series of velvety, watery horizontal swatches, reddish or even maroon toward the bottom, modulating through pale yellows into blue-pinkish grays at the top. Watery, thin painted on unsized canvas so the colors feathered into one another, somewhat in the style of Morris Lewis's veils. Good old Lois! Abstract as it was, after a moment or so it became almost impossible to see the painting as anything other than a rendering of a moment during either sunrise or sunset.

"What's unfinished about that?"

"Wait," said Rennie, "this is only the background."

She led him to Lois's work table, took out a file folder and laid down a series of pencil sketches on onionskin, each one of hundreds of little black ticks carefully forming ethereal spirals, some swooping up, some down across the page, some in pairs like a double helix in motion.

"One of these or some combination of them is supposed to go over the colors, though how I can't yet tell. It's about the Zapatistas, you know."

"How's that?" Rufus bent and looked again, waited, perplexed.

"It seems down toward the jungle where the Zapatistas came from there's an ancient Mayan city called Toniná—"

"Yes. Very impressive place. You should see it."

"I want to. Seems also at some times of the year the swallows make up great swarms in the period when night is coming on. A 'murmuration' I guess it's called. It was a favorite thing of Lois's to go and witness, and Janice would take her."

"And that has to do with the Zapatistas how?"

"They came swarming up out of the jungle too, an army of Indians, a mass determined to confront the status quo. To liberate all of us. Janice points out that the middle class is always fearful of the 'masses,' the 'unruly mob' as they like to say. But not Lois. In her book the Zapatistas were as exciting and mysterious as those swallows down there."

ᄋᏠ

Then Rufus was back in Gainesville teaching all fall and it was five months, the beginning of the new year, before he could get back to Chiapas. At first he couldn't quite tell about Janice. Had she declined a little, become less sharp? Maybe. But then when he and the old girl went wandering through one of their evening-long conversations the vagueness dissipated, especially when there was some venom added to the mix. On Janice's shit list Evie Swift had assumed the number-one spot, so dominating that Janice had been forced to parole some of the lesser offenders such as Sandor, Petra Hobbs' husband.

'That man,' as she called him, had been summoned off to Rome to the bedside of his ailing mother, so Petra had taken the opportunity to sneak up the hill and sue for forgiveness. "She was pitiful," Janice said, "weeping and carrying on about how we'd loved one another for nearly a lifetime and at our age it wasn't the time to go breaking up a friendship like ours. I'm not sure I've loved Petra exactly that many years, but finally I had to let it all go and take her back," Janice said.

"So there were admissions on both sides?"

"What do you mean? Petra admitted that man had tried to screw me on the price for Lois's pictures. What else was there to admit?"

"Nothing, I guess."

She gave him her squinty, appraising eye, but didn't pursue the matter.

On to the perfidious behavior of Na Bolom, which turned out to be a kind of additional charge in the case against Evie Swift. Oh sure, the down payment on Lois's collection and Janice's negatives was paid, and right on time, the day before that show they put on for her in August at what she and Lois used to call Na Baloney. September? Yes, they coughed up then too. October? Late, and only half of what Janice was owed. The claim was with tourist season over they were running a little short. But they did send around a smooth-talking young Italian fellow named Jacobo who was purported to be an expert in art restoration and wanted to know what brands of paint Lois used. Why'd he want that information? she asked. Because he was about to begin cleaning Lois's paintings, he explained.

Then nothing. No November money, no more Jacobo, December nothing either. "I was screwed, wasn't I?" Janice said, a smile on her face. "Should have gone with those people of yours in Chicago, I guess. What was the name of the library?"

"The Newberry." Rufus suppressed the desire to say 'I told you.' But then he hadn't, had he? Told her.

According to Rennie, the day after the Na Bolom opening, Janice got Evie on the phone and demanded the return of Lois's diaries. When? That very day would not be too soon, she said. Evie dropped off five inch-thick black-covered journals that afternoon and, probably sensing a tempest was on the brew, didn't come in to say hello.

"What she doesn't know is that before I gave her those diaries I numbered them. Here, they're on the shelf right there. Bring 'em down, will you, I'll show you."

Rufus pulled himself out of his chair by the fire and brought her the books and Janice showed him a faint pencil "6" on the inside back cover of the bottom one. "Five! There is no Five!" she proclaimed triumphantly.

"Did you mention it to Evie?"

"I did better than that. Miguel Briceño is going to send her a letter noting that she is in receipt of stolen property and demanding she return it. That'll put the fear of God in her, don't you think?"

"Probably not."

"Well it should!"

The fifth volume. What could be in it? Notes from the rockiest time in their relationship? The nastiest things Lois had to say about Janice? The under-story of their perfect happiness?

Leakage. Leakage in old age. Having to try to defend your version of the past when you hardly have the strength left to get yourself out of bed of a morning and lumber about.

How easy it would be, Rufus could see, to become obsessed with what was going to happen to you--or how they were going to fuck with the story you were leaving--after you were gone. Toward the end of his own foreshortened life, Rufus's Javier sometimes got heavily into seeing what he might be able to micromanage from beyond the grave. Some of his demands were fun. On the invitations to his funeral he wanted the notation 'Natural fiber clothing only, please.' Others were nasty--his ashes to be strewn at midnight in the Little Havana park where he played as a child and, since he was furious at Rufus at the moment he got that idea, Rufus to be barred from being present.

☙

Rennie said Janice was all excited because she'd made contact with a man in Australia who said he was sure he could put her in touch with Lois. He conducted séances by telephone with people all over the world, and his rates were reasonable enough (about twenty dollars for fifteen minutes, credit cards accepted), but the long-distance charges were on the seeker, of course. It made Hannah Seiden nervous to see Janice's phone bills go up and up. She asked Rennie whether contact had been made yet or not, and Rennie told her at the most recent session the mystic had felt Lois present in the room with him in Perth, but she wouldn't quite settle down enough to come to the phone.

"Isn't it strange?" Rennie said. "I mean, a hard-headed old marxist like Janice, and I'm assuming Lois was something similar."

"It's a side of both of them not everybody knows," Rufus said. "They always used to put a lot of faith in the Ouija."

"They did?"

He nodded. "In fact, the board is still there, on the bottom shelf of that bookcase Buster sits up on top of. I saw it the other day."

"Did you play with them?"

"I would observe some, but I was generally excused from sitting at the table."

"Because?"

"Lois was convinced I was strangely lacking in any sort of mystical gifts and that I might well frighten off some of the more antsy *spirits.*"

☙

Because they'd need the wheelchair as well as the walker for the trip to Toniná, they engaged Guadalupe for the day. He was Janice's faithful regular *taxista* and he brought around his recently-acquired VW wagon with all the extra room. "Rufus up front and Rennie and me in back, alright?" Janice said. "If this is to be my last expedition, I may as well have things the way I want, shouldn't I?"

"As if you don't always."

"Get my way? Ha! If you think that, you don't know the half of it."

"Janice?" said Rennie, "I'd appreciate it if you'd stop calling this your <u>last</u> expedition. It sounds so dire."

"Does it? Of course. I'm sorry, Sweetie."

In three hours and a little they were in the parking lot beside the new museum at the archeological site. Toniná itself is about half a mile farther along down a hot dirt road and across a tree-lined creek. Janice said just leave her at the little refreshment stand halfway to the creek, she'd seen the place. Guadalupe got her wheeled in to a table in the shade and said he would stay and watch out for her.

The vast majority of Mayan pyramids seem to be stylized representations of mountains, many of them set in flat savannahs. What is different about Toniná, a city-state of long duration, is that it was built up the side of an actual mountain, and though there are pyramids of gray-brown stone along the way, it presents itself at first as a long—sometimes endless-seeming—set of steep steps and platforms. Visitors respond by wanting to climb, and the view from the top is exhilarating, pastures, orchards and fields of corn, distant mountain ranges, all in the saturated blue-green of the tropics, mottled shadows of hurrying passing clouds. Often hawks hover overhead, still or feathers only a little ruffled on the wind.

Janice passed the afternoon treating Lupe to <u>paletas</u> one after another—each time a different fruit flavor she wanted to try—until they each had five popsicle sticks and wrappers lined up on the table before them. Rufus and Rennie were later getting back than they had planned, and Janice was anxious. Rufus had thought they could view the spectacle they had come for from the refreshment stand, but Janice insisted they move. She directed Lupe back to the main road and along toward Ocosingo about a mile, then asked him to pull off at a break in the trees before a large fenced field.

Janice sat out in her wheelchair by the vehicle, as expectant as a child, looking left and right, then over her shoulder. The sun had just gone down behind them, coloring the sky yellow and then a rusty pink, but going quickly toward dusk. "I hope we haven't come at the wrong time," Janice said grimly, more to herself.

Then the swallows began to show up, first in ones and twos, zooming by almost too fast to catch an individual one with your eye. There was calling—was it calling to one another?--and more and more appeared. Rufus and Lupe stayed with Janice, but Rennie hurried out into the field where there were some Brahman cows grazing. They looked at her, moved a little, but didn't seem much concerned. And suddenly, the number of birds flocking in became huge. They flew into a tight formation—like a large hairball up against the sky, Rufus thought, laughing at himself for his inability to summon up a poetic thought at the poetic moment--and then began to disperse, a line, a thickening line going off left, then up, down, around. Thousands of swallows swooping and divebombing then wheeling and climbing together.

The initial thrill of it didn't last long. Rufus could feel himself withdrawing, becoming a mere spectator again. Rufus at the air show, he thought. Janice and Lupe were better, apparently staying with the phenomenon as it went on. You kept thinking the birds were done, but then like overlapping musical themes the swarming and the spiral rising and curling and crossing itself would come again. Later what Rufus remembered was that after the initial squawking or call to arms, a shushing of many wings would come and then silence would permeate the twilight.

When it finally seemed to be dissipating, fewer birds, Rennie called out from down in the field, "Oh Janice!"

Janice took a little hanky out of her pocket, wiped her eyes, blew her nose.

"You been crying, Sweetie?"

"A little," she said.

"About?"

"Oh—" she looked up at Rufus and even in the half-light he could see her eyes were rimmed red, "—because I'm such a fool."

"How's that?"

"To have fallen in love with that girl!" She stuck her chin out in Rennie's direction. "At my age! But I couldn't help myself, you know? I'm not in charge."

"No, of course not. You know she loves you too."

"She does? You think?"

"I do."

"But not exactly in the same way."

"Maybe not."

The swallows had all dispersed and nightfall was near. Rennie came tromping back up toward them through the weeds. Janice pulled herself more upright and released the brake on her chair. Lupe sprang to and wheeled her over to the VW.

"I had the funniest dream," Janice said cheerfully. "Tell me what you think. We were in the afterlife together, Lois and I. But she'd undertaken an affair, just plunk gone off with somebody else. I knew I could get her back, I wasn't worried about that part, but I kept thinking 'How the heck can she be so unfaithful to me? To <u>us</u>!' It's not that I'm being unfaithful to her just because these thoughts about Rennie keep cropping up, is it?"

Rufus thought.

"Well, I guess you're right, it is, isn't it?" Janice said. "Unfaithful."

ᘓ

For Maryanne, 'How many times will I have to return?' began to be a somewhat burdensome question. Chiapas no longer called her as it did after Giles's death. Rosie Tu'ul

(Rosie <u>Utrillo</u> she had to remind herself) wrote to inform her her mother Losha had died and there seemed to be no other little old ladies Maryanne knew in Manantiales she would want to sit in the sweat bath and cackle over nothings with. At first it irritated her that Rosie's letter had taken six weeks to reach Wilmette. What kind of conspiracy did the U.S. and Mexican post offices have going? On which side of the border were the warehouses where they <u>stored</u> air mail before deciding to send some of it along?

But then the long interval began to seem a kind of kindness. By the time she got Rosie's letter Janice Metz had also died. Not that the news about Losha made her less sad than the news about Janice, but rather that coming on top of one another the two hard facts forced her back on old ideas about death she had not examined for some time. "Peanuts'" Charlie Brown, for example, and his fall obsession with trees shedding their leaves. In one strip he watched one leaf flutter down and then when a second one started after it, he said, "Here comes your buddy." Corny? She wasn't sure. Should there be an afterlife, which Maryanne was now pondering again, why wouldn't her two old friends become buddies? Especially once she got there and could introduce them.

What would the language of Heaven be?

And would Giles Fort be there, and if so would she still be married to him? She <u>had</u> begun to prize her new independence fairly seriously, might have some trouble giving it up. After all, what's a Heaven for if not as a place of freedom?

Hannah Seiden called a second time to say there was to be no funeral, but that Maryanne needed to come anyway. Janice's new lawyer from Tuxtla had let it out that Maryanne had been named executor of the will and he didn't want there to be any irregularities anyone could call upon later on so he needed her present when he unsealed the document. Hannah said, "I told Mr. Briceño I did not know how he could see all the way from Tuxtla that the buzzards are already lined up on the back fence here waiting to pick through Janice's stuff, and Mr. Briceño said, 'San Cristóbal is the <u>home</u> of the buzzards.'"

Maryanne did not make a hotel reservation. Guadalupe the *taxista* picked her up in sweltering Tuxtla, whisked her up the mountain through a cooling fog layer, plopped her bag out on the sidewalk at Janice's door and reached up to ring the bell in what felt like one long smooth gesture. Beta came running, all smiles for Maryanne before she remembered to put back on her solemn face.

There had been changes, the most striking being that the wall between the house and the casita was finally all gone. Shalik had managed somehow to integrate the two gardens so nicely it became hard to remember the wall had ever been there. In sweatpants and a hooded sweatshirt Rennie looked even taller than she did when she showed up at home in April sporting that buzz cut. Maryanne was reminded of the lanky girl she had been when she played volleyball at New Trier. How many years since anyone had thought of Rennie as 'lanky'?

Daughter had already put fresh sheets on her own bed for her mother. She herself planned to take her sleeping bag in to the long divan in Lois's room, which was where Lois would sit to get a longer look at whatever she had on the easel across the room. Rennie acted as though she knew Lois well, though Maryanne calculated their last interactions had been when Rennie had just graduated from kindergarten. But maybe she retained some memory of the ladies as they were back then. Janice and Lois usually doted on small children and plied them with cookies.

The bed in the casita was big and comfortable, ten inches of foam on a low plywood platform. Maryanne had some trouble going to sleep because of the ghostly bulbous eye of the skylight overhead. Through it you could see the black San Cristóbal sky and the stars. And although Rennie was painting mainly with tempera, she was also making some oils and the casita smelled of pigment and turpentine. The floors along the walls in both rooms were lined with her new pictures. Rennie was a little apologetic about the number of them, but what Maryanne could see didn't seem to need apology. They were bright and abstract, some maybe a little slapdash but all of them certainly exuberant. Rennie said Janice had told her if she was serious she must work every day except holidays, although thinking about what you were doing also came under the heading of 'work.' "So," Rennie said, "I tried that and at least for me that seems to be a good way."

About four a.m. the sustained squeaking of the garden door brought Maryanne fully awake. It was Rennie. "Mom, OK if I come get in with you?"

"Sure. What happened? Get spooked over there?"

"No, not really."

Maryanne moved over, leaving Rennie the warm spot she had made for herself. They lay side by side, both alert. Rain had begun, tap-tapping lightly against the skylight and—a different, flatter sound—against the clay roof tiles.

"Do you remember about Janice's vision?"

"I didn't even know she'd had visions."

"I asked her and she said only once had she ever had one, and it was an odd one at that. Remember the fireplace in her bedroom, the one she never used?"

"Vaguely, yes, I guess."

"Well Janice said one night she was entirely awake lying in bed and suddenly she saw what looked like a solid gold right-angle standing on the mantel of that fireplace and glowing, giving off light. Entirely perfect, she said, so beautiful it made her want to cry. Then slowly it began to move, down to the end of the mantel and then back to the middle. She couldn't believe it, she said. She pinched herself to make sure she wasn't dreaming, but she wasn't. So she just lay there and watched it and the tears ran down her cheeks, and then after a while it began to glow less and then finally it went away. And that was it, Janice's only vision."

Maryanne thought for a moment. "Interesting that Janice was a draftsman (or 'draftsperson'? you don't suppose they say that now, do you?) and her 'vision' isn't saints or angels or even little children holding hands around the world, it's a vision out of plane geometry."

"I thought of that. But Mom, I saw it too, just now."

"The right angle? But you were in Lois's room."

"Yes. It wasn't resting on anything, it was just there on the wall."

"And did it move, like it did for Janice?"

"Yes. Straight off to the left, then back to center."

"And then did it fade?"

"I don't know. Maybe. Losing energy. But then I suddenly decided I needed my mommy."

"Should we go look and see if I can see it too?"

"No. I don't see why. Besides, it's nice in here, isn't it?"

Rennie rolled to her, her body touching Maryanne's, arm loosely over her mother's waist. "Mom?"

She could feel Rennie's breath against her own cheek when she spoke. "What?"

"I just wanted to thank you for giving me Janice."

"She had things for you, didn't she?"

"Lessons, yes. A lot of them."

"Ones I couldn't give you."

"Don't say that. I wasn't about to listen to you anyway, was I? All that hostility I was putting out. Big waste, huh?"

"Do you have any idea where it was coming from?"

"I sometimes think I was resentful because my own father seemed to want me to be a fuck-up."

"Giles? Oh. He never--"

"No, listen. The other three are all such big successes in their way—Junior in his practice, the girls with their high-earner husbands and their kids in those snotty private schools. And you know it turned Dad off some, as though all that yuppy stuff they bought into reflected badly on him and you, your values. So to have at least one child who was 30 years of age still sponging off you guys, no secure job from year to year and, let's be honest, no clue—"

"Honey," Maryanne said calmly, "I don't think your father ever wanted you to fail."

"But if I was a failure as a painter, wouldn't that bear out his belief that no Fort was going to make it in the arts?"

"Maybe. But I know as a fact your father hated seeing you as miserable and indecisive as you were."

"OK. But isn't it a little weird how quick it all began to turn around for me once he was gone?"

Maryanne thought about it. The rain had blurred the skylight so you could no longer see the night sky. But after a bit, it did seem that the dome had changed, become moonstone gray, first hint of dawn. Maryanne found what she wanted to say, but then she listened and Rennie had gone to sleep, her mouth open a little bit and her breath shushing gently on the exhale.

CB

Round, fast-moving Licenciado Briceño came bustling in at ten the next morning in his worn suit, swinging his briefcase and followed by two little daughters, bespectacled shy creatures who sat at Janice's dining table with their noses in story books while their father conducted a reading of Janice's *testamento*. Those the lawyer had summoned were Maryanne, Rennie, Beta, Shalik the gardener, and Hannah Seiden. Maryanne was named *albacea* or executrix, nothing surprising there except the term, which she had never heard before. Translated into gringo dollars, the bequests would seem small, ten thousand pesos to Beta and ten thousand for Hannah, eight thousand for Shalik. But no one seemed disappointed. They all knew Janice had spent up a lot of her savings on the air ambulance and her operation in Houston, and besides the will contained nice little accolades to each of them for the ways they had cared for her. Shalik and Beta both cried.

The will also mentioned that it was Janice's understanding that Rufus Bright did not need any financial reward for his friendship, but he could have as many of the books in the house as he would like to take.

The only big surprise? Janice leaving Rennie the house.

And the thorn she left for the executrix to deal with? Maryanne was instructed never to allow Evgenia Swift (also known as 'Evie' and 'Gini' the document said) to set foot inside the premises again under any circumstances, the interdiction to remain in place no matter to whom ownership of the property passed. Unenforceable, surely, as Sr. Briceño mentioned. Then he apologized. He had been faint-hearted and unable to raise objections with Janice while she was spelling out her last wishes.

☙

Several days went by before the full impact of Janice's gift began to get through to Rennie. She had been worrying about where she'd go when she was forced to vacate the casita and how she was going to maintain herself now that the money she'd brought in the beginning and the birthday cash from her mother had been used up.

"Well, you know you were costing your father and me about six thousand dollars a year in therapy bills before," Maryanne said. "What if I keep up payment at about the same level? Then in my own small way I could think of myself as a patron of the arts."

Later, when she came by, Hannah Seiden said, "If you move into the main house, you'll have what the casita rents for. Or you could do it the other way around: keep the casita yourself and rent out Janice and Lois's. That way you'll be able to keep Beta."

"Oh," Rennie said. "Just for me?" She reddened at the thought. "I shouldn't do that."

"Think about it, dear. Do you want to have to spend your mornings going over to the market and the rest of the day cooking and cleaning up after yourself? And besides, Beta has her child to think of. What kind of employment do you imagine she'll find if she can't work for you?"

"But still—"

Maryanne sat that one out, her eye on the two younger women. Even though there were humongous new supermarkets down at the bottom of town with freezers full of TV dinners, Hannah was right. If you didn't want to eat out all the time, feeding yourself in SanCris remained time-consuming. How clever of the early gringo settlers, socialists and communists alike, to find a place where even the most impecunious of foreigners could afford a maid. And a gardener.

☙

One more time.

It was three months later, toward the end of fall. Old Don Ángel had finally finished carving the inscription and Maryanne felt she needed to be present for the placing of Janice's stone. The date chosen was during the same week that would mark Lois's hundredth birthday. Greta Contreras announced that immediately following the ceremony at the house she would be putting on a luncheon at the Alhambra to celebrate the lives of her two old friends, Janice and Lois, and that everyone was invited.

Though Maryanne preferred being in the casita, Rennie was working there in the morning, so it was more convenient for Maryanne to read or do whatever in the main house living room. When she came in, both cats roused suddenly and looked up, probably still hoping it might be Janice. They were less watchful when it was Beta returning from the market with her basket.

Maryanne was treated to a steady stream of visitors coming by the house for no apparent reason. It took her a while to figure out that what they really wanted was to find out how she was planning to deal with Evie Swift should Evie have the nerve to show up for the stone-laying. The decision was certainly Maryanne's, the artist Mitzi said, and she didn't envy her having to make it. Herself, she wouldn't know what to do. Others brought scraps of information obviously meant to affect the situation one way or another. Some thought the missing diary was missing because it had never existed except in a poor old woman's paranoia about what her lover said behind her back. But Greta claimed the book had been in Evie's possession when she walked through the Alhambra lobby one day. She, Greta, had seen it! It was black, wasn't it?

Rufus Bright asked could he come begin looking through Janice and Lois's library. Maryanne arranged it so she was out during the noon hour and left Rennie to deal with him. But when she returned he was still there, occupying what seemed like a lot of the sala, a tower of four or five books he had taken out of the shelves stacked on the dining table. Maryanne found herself being civil, even pleasant.

"This might interest you," he said. "I thought I had all the Janice photos I really coveted, but then I realized there was one I was missing. It's a fiesta in Chenalho' I think, crosses, a crowd, a man dancing, a lot of fire and a lot of smoke."

"Oh, I know that one. We put it in the show," Rennie said.

"Right. Well, so I called and asked Evie Swift if she had a print of it and she said she did. So I went by, and she brought out one of Janice's photo paper boxes and there were several copies of the one I wanted, all fresh and beautifully meticulously printed by the master herself, and Evie said I could have any one of them I wanted. For how much? Four hundred dollars, she said. She must have seen the look on my face, since that was double what Janice ever charged me. 'I need to eat too, you know,' she said. 'And I'm not getting any younger either.'"

Rennie said, "Well that might explain one thing."

"What's that?"

"Beta says that when she came to work the day following Janice's death the front door had been left unlocked. We thought maybe it was our mistake, getting the body removed from the house and all. But then I also found some of Janice's photographs were not where I thought they were."

"Didn't they all go to Na Bolom?"

"The negatives did. But Janice held back some of her own prints. They were in boxes under her bed. She said they were never part of the deal she made."

"And you think what Evie showed me might be among those."

"She did have a key to the house at one point."

Rufus put his books into a net bag he had brought with him. Then turned to Maryanne. "So what are you going to do tomorrow?"

"About Evie? I still haven't made up my mind," she said. "I'm more or less hoping she won't show up."

ℭ

They gathered under the big tree at the foot of the property at noon, twenty or so of them, a somewhat larger crowd than Maryanne had expected. Beta and Shalik and Sr. Briceño and the usual resident or semi-resident gringos, Amelia Olmsted, Petra Hobbes but no Sandro. And no Evie Swift.

At first the only sensation, if there was to be a sensation, was Mitzi bringing with her a tall, diffident young man in slacks and a V-neck sweater. The son of Shalik, Janice's gardener, he worked as a stock boy at a grocery store downtown and was taking courses at the local branch of the UNAM. Though some people had hoped scandal might attach to the liaison of a white woman and an Indian man, apparently that era had passed and except for the thirty-year age difference between them there seemed to be nothing for tongues to wag about. Rufus Bright said he felt like the godfather to the relationship, since he was the one who had encouraged Mitzi to get to know some people from Chamula better.

No speeches had been planned and no blessings, although there were some candles placed around among the impatiens surrounding the tree. Maestro Don Ángel kept his fresh-cut piece of granite off to the side under a cloth. Shalik had made a hole about two feet deep beside Lois's stone and when Maryanne asked her to Hannah Seiden came forward and placed the metal box with Janice's ashes snugly in the bottom. Shalik shoveled dirt in until there was only a small indentation and then with a little flourish Don Ángel whipped the cloth off the marker and with a grunt managed to pick it up. He staggered over and let the irregular block down in, evoking a collective sigh from those watching.

Janice's birth date and death date and the same geometric flowers that Lois's stone had. The same somewhat unsettling mix of upper- and lower-case letters as well. Janice's marker looked only a little cleaner and brighter than her beloved's.

And then there was Evie, hurrying down on them all in black, holding a floppy straw hat to her head. Stopping, she said to Maryanne, "I'm so sorry, I <u>did so</u> not want to be late for this!"

Maryanne said, "We're glad you could come, Evie." Which netted her hard looks from several of the bystanders. So she was going against the old girl's wishes. So what? Was she a softer, more forgiving person than Janice? She didn't think she was, but Evie Swift was not exactly her battle either.

She and Beta had discussed whether there should be coffee or tea or something after the setting of the stone, but because of the luncheon downtown to follow, they had decided against it. People stood for a while contemplating the two stones, having their thoughts, chatting, and then began trooping back up toward the house.

Maryanne and Rennie got jackets and started out down the hill toward the Alhambra. When they got to the little plaza in front of the Casa de Pan, Maryanne could see several of those who had been to the setting of the marker trundling off down streets that led away from the center of town. In the hotel lobby no one from their group except Rufus and Patrick Durban,

Janice's old tenant who happened to be back in San Cristóbal for just a few days.

Greta met them and led them up into the restaurant. The tables were made up with napkins and silverware and decorated with bowls of yellow and brown alstroemeria, and the long counter at the end of the room was all laid out with the usual chafing dishes and platters of the hotel's buffet. Two plump women in hairnets stood ready to serve and the dining room manager in his dark suit hovered.

"I have no idea where everyone is," Greta said. She pulled out chairs and got the four of them seated at one table, but then the front desk came to fetch her to the phone. Some problem with one of the established tours booked in for next week, it seemed.

"Are we to be it, then?" Patrick Durban asked, looking around.

"Think so," said Rufus. "The invitation went out first by email and everyone was delighted. But then a couple days ago hard copy arrived in their mailboxes and they noticed at the bottom the card said, 'In honor of Lois and Janice the Alhambra is pleased to offer guests a reduction on the regular cost of our buffet of 15 percent.' And everyone thought, 'Well fuck! Good old Greta, out to make a buck as always,' and decided not to come."

Greta had asked Maryanne to say something after the luncheon, so she had written some thoughts down on a 3 x 5 card. It was in her purse, but now there'd be no reason to take it out. One note said, 'Why go on a Tuesday?' which Maryane planned to mention not only because Janice <u>had</u> died on a Tuesday, but also because it might serve as a little dig at Evie Swift should she manage to show up for the luncheon.

But Evie hadn't.

When she got up at the end of the meal, Maryanne made a last little tour of the largely untouched array of delicious dessert things on the buffet counter. Only one or two pieces missing from the apple tart with almonds and the dense iced chocolate cake, and one scoop out of the big bowl of custard.

The manager picked up a paper napkin, spread it open across his palm and raised his cake knife. "Wouldn't you like a little of the chocolate here to take with you, Señora?" he asked.

Maryanne laughed and said, "Well, I don't <u>need</u> any extra cake, thank you."

"Señorita Janice always took an extra piece to eat later."

"Did she? Well cut me one too then, will you?" Maryanne said.

Made in United States
North Haven, CT
12 October 2023

42692341R00128